RESCUE MAN

P.J. Patterson

For Nate and Katie...my shooting stars.

one

"**D**r. Thompkins?" Will Thompkins was putting on his jacket getting ready to leave his office as the intern looked up at him nervously.

"I have to be out of here by six…what is it?"

"The EMTs are on their way with a head injury, a pedestrian struck by an SUV at high speed, found unresponsive at the scene. The coma score is 5T, right eye is fixed and dilated. He was intubated in the field. We can't find Dr. Chang…"

"Pulse?"

"Pulse is 50, BP is 180 over 100."

"Get neurology down here and page Dr. Chang, I think she's at dinner.

Tell radiology we'll need a head CT and notify surgery. Has the family been contacted?"

"There was no ID, the police are working on it. It's a nine-year-old boy..."

Will winced. He stood motionless for a moment, then pulled off his jacket and reached for his scrubs. "Okay, notify pediatrics too. I'll go meet the EMTs."

Pediatric trauma cases sent everyone in the ER into a hyper-emotional state. You could get jaded, even cocky about the daily parade of adult patients filing through a city emergency room like Mercy Hospital—drug overdoses, heart attacks, gunshot wounds, car accidents. But children were a different story. Children were supposed to be off-limits. Children were supposed to be at the schoolyard kicking around soccer balls, at home dreaming in their beds. When a pediatric trauma case came in, your guard went down, you lost your swagger. You got reminded how fragile life is. You prayed that your own kids were home safe in their beds.

Will gathered his team and went over the protocols, trying to neutralize their anxiety. He made a point of speaking in a calm, steady voice, the same voice that would be giving them orders when the ambulance arrived.

When the paramedics burst into the hallway and pulled off the blankets, he saw the boy. He was lying like a broken bird on the gurney, his skinny arms and legs shattered and splinted, his face bruised and swollen with blood, the intubation tube in his throat. A Red Sox t-shirt, cut away by the paramedics, was lying bunched beside him. Will paused to allow himself a split-second to register the heartache of the scene, to remember that there was a parent, a sibling, a best friend who loved this boy, who did not know yet that his life was hanging by a thread, that his fate was in the hands of doctors they had never met. He did this each time he faced a patient—and he made every doctor who served under him do it—so that he never got immune to the suffering of the souls before him. Then he went into action, examining the boy tenderly as he gave orders, trying to mitigate the injuries until neurology arrived.

"Give half a mg of mannitol, a head CT stat, X-rays, CBC, chemistries, type and cross for 6 units FFP and blood products. Get 14 pack platelets on call for the OR…"

When he was treating trauma patients Will went into a heightened reality, where his mind worked smarter and faster, where he could see and analyze a dozen things at once, calling out orders, his hands moving quickly, gently, as if they were guided by another force.

He talked quietly to the boy as he dressed his wounds—about baseball and school and his favorite movies—the same soft patter he always used to distract patients in pain. He never assumed a patient couldn't hear him. He talked over their bodies as though it were a benediction. He wanted the boy to know that they were working to fix him, working to relieve his suffering. So much of pain is tied up in fear.

It was a devastating injury. His only chance for recovery was immediate surgery and removal of the blood that was putting pressure on his brain; without surgery he would die. Even with it, chances were high that he would have neurologic injury, or die on the table.

The neurosurgeon and pediatrician arrived, and Will turned it over to them as he watched the boy being wheeled off. He looked at his watch—6:30. He thanked his team, assuring them they did everything they could, and went back to his office, standing quietly for a moment, taking a deep breath as the adrenalin began to leave his body. Then he removed his scrubs, put on his jacket, and headed home to his own children.

two

"How do I look?

Lee glanced up from the kitchen table where he sat in a sprawl of pizza and paper plates. A scrawny five-year-old, her mouth covered in pizza sauce, was propped in his lap. He looked at his friend standing expectantly before him, his face etched with worry, as though some fresh new disaster was poised to strike him at any moment.

"You look good. Like you just escaped from prep school." Lee said, eyeing the cadet blue sweater and slacks suspiciously.

"I'm trying to look like a responsible parent."

"You do, just not from Berkeley."

"You look pretty, Will." The five-year old offered. She was dangling a slice of pizza, the cheese sliding its way toward the floor as the dog waited patiently for the spoils.

"Thank you, baby. Why aren't you finishing your dinner? We have to go soon, Danny's already dressed, you're still in your slip."

"I'm not hungry." She leaned back into Lee's lap wrapping her legs around him.

Lee retrieved what was left of the pizza and folded it in half. "Here you go, one more big bite." She scrunched up her face and bit reluctantly. Before she could finish swallowing he wiped her mouth clean with a sweep of paper towel. "Okay, you better go upstairs and get dressed. She untangled herself and meandered out of the kitchen.

"Why are you so worried about this? They already got in, stop obsessing, everything's going to be fine."

"It's my first time meeting the head of the school, I want to make a good impression. She could still change her mind, you know." He was shifting back and forth on the balls of his feet as if he was ready for a fight.

"Didn't we meet her at open house? Dark hair, nice ass?"

"Yes, but she didn't know who we were then, this is a one-on-one. And by the way, nice way to make a good impression— my best friend hitting on the head of the school."

"They're terrific kids, you're a respectable doctor, she's not going to change her mind. And stop looking so desperate, women hate that." Lee could see a wave of panic ripple across Will's face. "Do you want me to go with you? 'Cause I'm perfectly happy to go."

Will entertained the idea, scanning his friend slouched on the chair in his turquoise Hawaiian shirt and cargo shorts.

"Like *that*? No, geeze. They'll think we're a gay couple—and I'm the 'neat' one. No, I'll be okay, really, I don't need you this time."

"Okay, then, breathe. Everything is going to be fine." Lee felt as if he had spent most of the previous year repeating that same phrase, like a mantra, hoping it would have the power to stitch up the gaping wound in his friend.

Will looked at his watch and called up the stairs. "Jules, Dan, let's go!" After a few minutes they came bounding down.

"I'm ready!! Lee, look at my new dress!" Jules twirled in front of him.

"It's beautiful baby, you look like a plaid princess." Lee turned to the little boy standing quietly, his hand dug deep into Will's pocket holding on against any onslaught of hurt. The whole family was so wounded, he thought, some days you could hear the wind blowing through their hearts.

"Dan, my man, look at those new clothes! You look way cool, just like Will. You're like a family of little Republicans." Will was patting down the boy's curls in a futile attempt to tame them into a part.

"What's a republican, Will?"

He cupped his hands tenderly over both their heads and navigated them toward the front door. "Never mind, you can't find them in Berkeley."

Lee bent down to kiss them both. "Okay, go knock 'em dead at school. I'll see you when you get back. And you," he clamped his hand firmly on Will's shoulder, "they're in, relax. *Everything's going to be fine.*"

They stood huddled in the office doorway, a triptych of anxiety.

"Welcome, Mr. Thompkins, come in," a tall, tailored woman gestured Will inside, shaking his hand. She was wearing a slim black skirt and a sweater with a wide belt. She did have a great ass. Damn Lee.

"Juliana and Daniel, I'm pleased to see you, have a seat." The three of them shuffled toward three waiting chairs, the children with their hands still latched deep in Will's pockets. They had gotten to moving around this way so often that Lee called them the six-legged monster. Dan and Jules avoided the chairs, huddling next to Will. "Is Mrs. Thompkins going to be joining us…or a significant other?"

Will's stomach became a ball of rubber bands. *Strike one.*

"No, I'm not married actually, it's just me…well, there's my brother, Dave, but he's in Boston doing his surgical internship, so it's pretty much just me… oh, and our nanny, Maria, she's been with the family for years. She takes care of the kids when I'm at work." Will scanned the face of the woman for signs of disapproval. She didn't seem to register any emotion at all. He thought she was probably conditioned to do this so there wasn't a scene. In a few days a disembodied letter would arrive in the mail politely rejecting them.

"I see." She put on her glasses and began to look over the folder of papers in front of her. "Alright, then let's get started. As I said over the phone, the children did well on their academic tests. There are a few notes here about socialization, but we can talk about that another time."

Will tried to calm himself down by breathing deeply into his diaphragm, the way he had practiced with the therapist, but he could feel the panic flooding into his chest.

"Will, I'm cold," Jules whispered in his ear. Her breath was small and hot. He reached over and buttoned her sweater and rubbed her arms to warm her up, keeping his eyes on the woman so as not to appear disengaged. When he glanced down at Jules he saw that he had missed two button holes at the top and the whole sweater was flapping crazily askew.

"The first thing I'd like to talk about is that we've put the children in separate classes. We find this is good for twins, it gives them a chance to individuate, spread their wings."

Will's body went numb. He felt Dan and Jules tense up, digging their hands deeper into his pockets, pushing their little bodies up against him. He wrapped his arms around them and pulled them in close, the three of them now a single, massive ball of rubber bands. "Oh, no…I don't think you understand, they can't be split up."

"Will, I'm *freezing*…" Jules looked up at him plaintively. Her teeth were chattering. He frantically pulled his navy sweater up over his head and put it on her, rolling up the sleeves to free her hands. From the corner of his eye he saw that his shirt had a pizza stain on it.

"I know many parents of twins feel that way, Mr. Thompkins, so let me explain our thinking…"

"No, there's no *thinking*, Ms. Harkins." Will heard his voice rise into an unfamiliar raspy falsetto. He tried to stand up, but Jules had wrapped herself around his leg in a wrestling hold so he could only manage to tilt to one side. "I'm sure you have very good reasons under normal circumstances, but after everything they've been through they *can't* be separated…they just can't…I thought I made that clear in my letter." His mind raced…*there was always public school.* He felt the disapproving stare of his grandmother. He saw his children, tattooed and surly, slouched out on the blacktop, smoke rings of marijuana wafting from their pierced lips…

"Oh, Mr. Thompkins, I don't think I've seen your letter," The woman began to shuffle through the papers. "I apologize, it seems to have been misplaced." The air flowed into his lungs again. He looked down at his children to see they had transformed back into navy blue and plaid republicans.

"Oh, no, don't apologize, that makes much more sense. Hang on a minute." He released their little hands from the death-grip on his pockets and stood both children in front of him. "Can you guys go get two cups of water for me and Ms. Harkins?" There's a water cooler right around the corner in the hallway…careful not to spill." They nodded and scrambled out the door, eager for an assignment. Will looked across the table to the expectant face of the woman. He winced, anticipating the pain as if he was about to jump off a curb onto a sprained ankle. "What I explained in my letter is…last year my parents were killed in an accident." A dull pain knifed its way along the familiar route, through his groin and up to his chest making it hard to breathe.

The woman gasped. "Oh…I'm so sorry Mr. Thompkins, I had no idea. Their grandparents…"

"No, *our* parents. Jules and Dan are my siblings. I have custody of them since my parents' death…it was all explained in the letter."

The room suddenly felt cavernous. Will heard himself babbling to fill the silence. "It's been a tough year, you know, they've had pretty severe separation anxiety—they've been in therapy, we've *all* been in therapy. It was a lot of heartbreak to navigate. You might have read about my parents—Henry Thompkins and Maria Gambiari? They were pretty well known in Berkeley. My father was a history professor at Cal, and my mother was a musician…" It was futile to try to sum up their lives—their brilliance and crazy affection for each other, the raucous dinners, the camping trips, the endless stream of friends and intellectual debates, the sound of his mother's violin singing through the house while he did his homework at the kitchen table…his parents' elation when they learned his mother was pregnant again with twins. He let himself swim in a sea of happy memories for a moment before he pulled himself back to the little office and the stunned face of the woman in front of him.

"How tragic, I'm so sorry, Will." Her face softened. "I apologize for the confusion. I agree completely the children should be kept together. That certainly explains why the teachers noticed that they had some…separation issues."

Separation issues. That was an understatement. Whenever either of them were out of his sight, Will became wracked with worry. He had lost forever the blissful illusion that the world was safe. At night he would lie in bed in a cold sweat imagining a tsunami of evil scenarios poised to wash over them, the anxiety rising in his throat until he felt as though he was choking. Only when their little bodies were near him would his mind drift into peaceful stillness, lulled by their voices, or the soft, rhythmic sound of their breathing which had now superseded his own.

He was jolted out of his thoughts by the noisy sound of Jules and Dan coming back into the room, each carefully balancing a cup of water in both hands. He felt his mood lift as he watched them eagerly pass around the paper cups.

"Thank you, I needed that," he said, drinking the cool water from the cup. The woman drank too, thanking them for a job well done, and the atmosphere in the room lightened as they resumed discussing the ordinary business of teacher assignments and test scores.

"Will, I'm still cold," Jules tugged at his sleeve. Will could see that now her whole body was shivering and she looked pale. He felt her cheek—she was hot...*a perfect ending to the night.* He suddenly felt exhausted.

"I'm sorry...I better take her home. Can we continue this later?" He gathered Juliana up in his arms, deflated.

"Of course. I think we've settled all the important issues." She stood up to see them out. "We'll be sending out the welcome packet with room assignments and class schedules."

Will stalled in the doorway. "We're...still in, right?"

"You're *in.*" She cupped her hand on his arm and gave it a squeeze. "And we're going to take good care of them, Will, I promise. They're going to be happy here."

"That's great. We're fourth generation Berkeleyans, you know—we live right in the neighborhood, over on Avalon. So we'll see you in September then...?"

"We'll see you all in September." And she watched as the six-legged monster lurched its way out into the night.

"Hey, you're back early...how did it go?

"Don't ask. It was a disaster."

"Why? Are they still in?"

"She was going to put them in separate classes. The letter got lost. She didn't know the story, I had to fill her in."

"Oh Jesus, that's unbelievable. Did she fix it? "

"Yeah, I...you know...explained the situation."

"That's it then?"

"Yeah, except five minutes into the meeting Jules got sick, she's got a fever. I think it's her ears. She threw up 30 seconds after we walked out of the office."

"I threw up on my new dress Lee." She looked miserable.

"And on my new sweater, which I put on her because she was cold."

"Well the sweater wasn't much of a loss."

"What about my dress, Lee?"

"We'll get that all fixed up, no worries. That'll wash right out. Come on, let's get you up to bed and check out those ears." She took his hand and walked listlessly by his side. He felt the tiny bones in her wrist as he held her. She was so fragile, he thought, how was she ever going to make it through all this. He reached down and lifted her to carry her up the stairs to bed. She wrapped her legs around his waist and rested her head against his chest; she felt almost weightless.

"There's amoxicillin in the medicine cabinet." Will called out from below. "From the last time."

"Got it," Lee called back. He was starting to feel the weight of the last year in his bones.

Will sat on the edge of Dan's bed scanning for signs of worry in his face. He was the kind of kid who'd fall off his bicycle and tell you he was fine, and an hour later you'd find him in his room with a welt the size of a baseball. It seemed to Will that the boy's single goal was to not cause anyone worry; he'd made up his mind that so much sadness permeated everyone in the house he wasn't going to add to the burden.

"You're quiet tonight, buddy. Everything okay?

"When are we going to our new school?"

"Not for a few months yet. In September."

"Are you sure I get to be in the same class as Jules?"

"Yes you do, babe, you *do* get to be in the same class as Jules, that was a total misunderstanding. Is that what you're worried about?" He nodded. "That was just a mistake, you're going to be together, so don't worry. Okay? I promise."

The boy reached up and put his thin arms around Will's neck and hugged him as though he was hanging on for life. Will rocked him back and forth in the bed to soothe him. "Everything's going to be fine. How about we go to the park tomorrow and ride the steam train. Sound good?" Dan lit up a bit. Will tucked the covers around him and kissed him. "Sleep tight...don't let the bedbugs bite." He tickled him through the covers until he was giggling. "Night, buddy."

He crossed into Jules' room to find Lee had already put her to bed. She was asleep, flushed and feverish, curled up in her favorite pajamas, images of Barbie cavorting across her tiny frame in friezes of youthful abandon. Barbie shopping, Barbie at the beach, Barbie roller skating with her friends. Where were Barbie's parents while she was having all this fun, he wondered? Maybe that's why Jules loved Barbie so much, she existed in a world without parents. Will kissed her hot cheek and made his way downstairs.

"I need a drink." Lee was already pouring scotch into two glasses.

"I'm way ahead of you."

"How is Jules, was it her ears?"

"Yeah. Not as bad as last time. But we've got to get her weight up…" As soon as the words came out of his mouth Lee regretted them.

A pang of guilt sliced through Will. *Failure to thrive*, the pediatrician said. It was a straightforward enough diagnosis when he was in med school, now it seemed like an indictment against him. *Failure to thrive.* She'd lost interest in eating since his parents died. She was already almost a full head shorter than Danny, a frail wisp of a kid you could pick up with one arm.

Will sank into his chair. "Do you think my life is ever going to be easy again?"

"No." Lee handed him the glass. "But you've got *them.* That still makes you lucky."

Will took a big swallow of scotch and felt the warmth ease into his chest. "It's a long way from med school days."

"That it is," Lee smiled. "Imagine explaining my living situation to one of *those* women. 'Why don't you come up to my place, I live with two little kids, their Latina housekeeper and my best friend in the house he grew up in. My bedroom is in the attic, so you have to be quiet during sex, because the kids are right below me.'"

Will laughed and felt a wave of gratitude for his friend. "What are *you* going to do? I feel bad about you putting your life on hold for me."

"What have I got to complain about? I'm living rent-free in this big house ten minutes from the hospital paying off my med school debt and being fed by Maria—I'm in the lap of luxury."

"Except for a neurotic best friend and the occasional throw-up of two five year olds."

"You know what, I'm crazy about these kids. If I didn't love sex with women so much I'd just move in and we could be one big gay happy family. Besides, let's be honest, I needed some domestic sanity. My personal life was getting a little out of control—in case you forgot the 'Tiffani incident.' Coming home to find your apartment spray-painted with obscenities by a bat-shit crazy stripper helps you rethink your priorities, believe me. It's not a good look for a doctor."

"Don't forget the restraining order."

"Five-foot-three, 110 pounds, the biggest thing about her was her implants, and I had to ask for a restraining order... *that* was a moment of reckoning."

Will fell silent, slumping deeper into the chair. He felt the familiar ache rise up in his throat as he remembered the last sight of his parents walking down the ramp to catch their flight, his mother's perfume still lingering where she had kissed him goodbye, his father clasping her tightly around her waist, grinning and waving back to him. He played the tableau over and over in his mind in a futile search for a rewind button that would let him rescue them from their pending fate.

"God, I miss my parents. I keep expecting them to walk through the door, like all of this has been a bad dream. My dad would just wave his hand and take charge and everything would be back the way it was."

Lee could see the pain start to swallow his friend.

"Let's go shoot some hoops."

"It's too late…"

"Come on old man, it'll take your mind off things. I'm getting flabby, I can use the exercise, let's go."

Will pulled his body out of the chair and headed out into the damp evening, to the makeshift basketball court his father installed when it became clear his bookish lifestyle was never going to suit his boisterous sons. As soon as he heard the basketball slap against the pavement, he felt his mood lighten. How many thousands of hours had they all logged, shooting hoops through this basket, hearing the metallic rattle of the backboard mounted above the garage as the ball hit it. When they were in high school and college they would start pick-up games that would last for hours into the foggy Berkeley evenings, with friends and neighborhood kids joining in. Afterward they would all pour into the big house, called in by the aromas of his mother's cooking. His father would protest that he was going broke feeding them all, and then hold court while they regaled him with their latest exploits as they sat around the big redwood table that dominated the old kitchen. The table, family legend had it, was a legacy of Will's great-great grandfather Thaddeus, who had hiked the Sierras with John Muir. After seeing a giant redwood felled by lightening, Thaddeus arranged to have the heart of it hauled to a carpenter to be made into a table for the family home. The tale was apocryphal, but Will loved it anyway, and he continued the tradition of telling Dan and Jules the story, exactly the way his father did, whenever they gathered around it. "This table is Mother Nature in all her raw power," he would say to their attentive little faces, spreading his hands across the beams of wood worn smooth from so many family gatherings. "She created this tree, and she took it down."

Slap, slap, slap, slap, the familiar rhythm began to lull Will. Maybe Lee was right. Maybe everything would be okay. The kids were doing better, even the therapist said so, and he was thriving in the ER. In the ER he was stronger, tougher—he was *fearless*.

"Find your true north," his father always told him, "that's what will make you happy." Henry Thompkins knew what he was talking about. He'd walked away from a life of privilege to pursue a career in academia, in spite of pressure to enter the family's business empire. "The road not taken," he would say wistfully. Slap, slap, slap...Lee came up from behind and jolted Will out of his reverie, stealing the ball out from under him and flinging it high in the air across the court for a basket. He grinned at his friend.

"Still got it."

Will smiled as the ball slipped easily through the hoop and bounced across the driveway onto a neighboring lawn.

"Hey, is the Lawson house going up for sale?" Lee was walking across the lawn toward a realtor's "Coming Soon" sign a few doors down the street. It pointed to a small craftsman-style bungalow nested among the grand old Tudors.

"Yeah, Carrie's parents moved to Florida, she's putting it up for sale."

"Really? How much do you think she wants for it?"

"I don't know, it needs a new roof... and I think the kitchen is pretty old."

"Who cares, I don't cook. Let's ask her." Lee's hands were cupped against the front window peering into the house.

"You mean you're interested?" Will was incredulous.

"Yeah, I'm interested. Why? Is that a surprise?"

"I don't know, I always pictured you living someplace, you know, *hipper.*"

"I love this neighborhood. This way I could be close to you and the kids."

"Be careful what you wish for, because they're crazy about you--they'll be knocking at your door every chance they get... me too probably."

"Do you think she'll give us a deal? I don't know if I have enough for a down payment."

Will scanned Lee's face trying to read him. He actually looked sincere. "I'll buy it with you...if you're serious. This house is paid for and I've got the insurance money to invest, I could use the write-off. You can buy me out later, once your practice gets going...if you're *really* serious." He eyed his friend with skepticism.

"I'm damned serious." Lee tucked the ball under his arm and headed for the house, waving Will in. C'mon, let's call Carrie. She always had a crush on you, maybe she'll give us a deal."

three

W ill remembered the precise moment he ceased to be an older brother. Maria had just finished putting out enchiladas for dinner. He was sitting at the kitchen table with Danny and Jules, and they were taking turns at the nightly ritual his father had instituted when he and Dave were kids: "What did you learn today?" Will recalled sometimes dreading coming to the big table on days when he couldn't think of a single thing to report, but his father always seemed to pull something out of him, and inevitably a lively discussion ensued with everyone noisily tossing in their opinions. He wanted to continue the tradition with his younger siblings, so each night the four of them, Lee often included, would sit around the old redwood table and make a game out of it. It satisfied Will to think that his father was still influencing his youngest children. This night, as he tossed out the challenge, Danny turned slyly to Maria.

"Maria, what did *you* learn today?" He grinned, catching her off guard.

"Oh, no, mijo" she laughed, "it's for *you!*"

Will looked at her with affection seated at the head of the table where his mother used to sit, her dark hair and soft, plump frame draped as always in a colorful printed dress she had sewn herself. She was the maternal, feminine force in the household now, and he had boundless gratitude for her presence. His mother hired her to help out when the twins were born, moving her into the small, shingled cottage behind the house, and the two women quickly became fast friends. The two Marias, his father called them as they giggled together over the antics of the children or clanged about the kitchen, singing and dreaming up new Mexican-Italian dishes to spring on the parade of visitors, friends and students that happily took refuge at the old redwood table.

Will was still haunted by the devastation he saw on her face the morning he knocked on the door of her little cottage to give her the terrible news. He'd been woken in the middle of the night with the call. For the first few minutes after he hung up the phone he was so disoriented he felt as though he was caught in some kind of surreal dream, as if there was still time to pull them back from death, before anyone knew, before it became real.

He waited as long as he could into the dawn to tell Maria, although he yearned for a companion to share his grief. When he finally told her, she dropped to her knees and began to keen softly and pray in Spanish. He instinctively dropped down to join her and they held each other, rocking back and forth--he didn't know for how long, since time no longer seemed real to him. When they were done, she collected herself and went to Danny and Jules, tenderly holding vigil over them throughout that awful day as friends and neighbors filed in and out of the house trying to navigate the business of death. Now Will couldn't imagine the house or his life without her soothing presence--her affectionate greeting when he came through the door after a long day in the ER, the dinners that brought them all to the table together, filling the air with aromas of Mexican spices and warm homemade tortillas. At night, when the children were fretful and couldn't sleep, Will would hear her singing soft Spanish lullabies to them and imagine she was singing to him too, the way his mother had.

"No, Danny's right. No one is exempt." Will teased. "What did *you* learn today, Maria?"

"Hmmm. Let me see…" She thought for a moment, taking the challenge to heart. "Ah, si, I have it. You know my sister, Margarita."

"Of course we know Margarita," Will said, amply familiar with the beloved sister Maria visited at her Gilroy farm nearly every weekend since she had come to work for his mother.

"Well Margarita's husband, Jorge, has a sister, Lupe, who lives still in Jalisco."

"Where you were born." Jules interjected.

"Si, niña, where I was born," Maria said proudly. "Now Lupe has a daughter named Esperanza, and Esperanza is married to Arturo, and Arturo's cousin, Artemisia, is getting married…a big wedding with all the family coming in the town. But Artemisia says she will not invite Lupe to the wedding, because

Lupe insulted her uncle Jesus, who is the assistant to the mayor of Jalisco, Antonio Ascencio."

The three of them sat in rapt confusion.

"Now Lupe is a…maker of the dresses…how do you say?"

"Seamstress." Will offered.

"Si, seamstress," Maria continued, "The best in all of Jalisco, and that is why Jesus asked Lupe to sew a dress for his wife Sobrilla for the celebration of the Virgin Mary on All Saints Day." At the mention of the Virgin, Maria crossed herself and glanced heavenward, both children dutifully following her. "But Lupe could not sew the dress, because she had too much work already to sew the dresses for the daughters of Emilio Castillo. This was not good, because Emilio Castillo is the opponent of Senor Ascencio in the election for Mayor. Lupe told Artemisia she was sorry, she had already promised the sewing for Senor Castillo's daughters—ah…Consuela and Christiana I think are their names. But Artemisia said she did not care, it was an insult to her family to sew dresses for Senor Castillo. And now Esperanza says if her mother cannot come to the wedding, she will not come, and Margarita says, that Jorge says if Lupe is not invited to Artemisia's wedding, Jorge will not go, and that means Margarita is not going either, even though she had set her heart to go and I sewed her a beautiful new blue dress for it with beads from here to here," she swept her hands across her breast to her hip for dramatic effect. "And now, Margarita is crying, and Lupe is crying, and no one is speaking to anyone." She folded her hands in front of her on the table and smiled with satisfaction. "And that is what I learned today."

The children looked at her wide-eyed.

"Wow, you learned a *lot,* Maria." Danny said.

"Si." She said, pleased with herself.

"How about *you* Will?" Danny decided to press his luck.

"Si, si, what did you learn today Dr. Will?" Maria said playfully.

Will shook his head and smiled. "Well, I learned that Maria has a very complicated family, and it's going to take me the rest of dinner to figure it all out." They all laughed and dove into their enchiladas.

Will noticed Juliana looking pensive. "You're being awfully quiet tonight, baby. What did you learn today?"

Juliana put her head down for a moment, thinking, and then looked up at Will.

"Are we orphans?"

The room became silent, except for a small gasp escaping from Maria. Will felt as though he'd been punched in the chest. Now both children were looking up at him, waiting for his answer.

"No," he said softly, trying to collect himself. Where did you hear that?"

"We saw a movie in school today about some kids in Africa, and it was called "Nobody's Children." They were orphans, because all of their parents died, and Kyle Harris said that Danny and me must be orphans too, because our parents died."

"You are *not* orphans,' Will said, his voice growing more emphatic. You *are* somebody's children, you're *my* children—I love you more than anything in this world. You have lots of people who love you, we're all part of a big family—Maria and Dave and Lee and your Grandmother. Do you understand? You are *my* children." And in that quotidian instant the realization struck Will—he had shape-shifted from big brother to father.

That night, after everyone had gone to bed, he lay awake staring into the darkness of his parent's bedroom, now his room. In the early weeks after the accident he had taken to sleeping there because it was closest to the kids' rooms—the same rooms he and Dave had occupied when they were growing up. At first he was uncomfortable in the big bed, that sacred spot his parents had retreated to every night and held as their fortress against four boisterous children, the very place where they had conceived those children in the passionate abandon they always had for each other. As a child he took refuge there when bad dreams sent him in search of comfort. He would climb up onto the big bed and lie between them while his mother stroked his hair and sang softly to him until he drifted off in the peaceful bliss of warm blankets and the scent of her skin. When he was older, it dawned on him just what was taking place behind that closed door, and the thought filled him with a mix of embarrassment and admiration for them. They were so effusively affectionate to each other, it made Will smile even now to think of it.

Now this was *his* bed, only empty, with none of the passion it once held, none of the comfort, only the dog and an occasional visit by two frightened children.

He lay there feeling the full weight of what had happened that night at dinner. *He was it—father, mother, brother, guardian, protector, savior.* It had all fallen on him.

They were *all* orphans, exposed, like starfish scattered on the beach, as the tide of their parents' love receded. The ache began to creep into his chest. He picked up the phone and called Lee.

"It's me. Are you busy?"

"I'm…entertaining."

"Got it. I'll call tomorrow."

"It's okay, she's in the shower, what's up?"

"I don't know…I'm kind of in crisis here."

"What happened?"

"It's a long story. Listen, we have a deal, total honesty, right?" It was a pact they made in med school that they could rely on each other to tell the truth, even when they had made a mistake.

"Right." Lee began to sense this was not an ordinary panic call, although such calls came frequently enough that he was practiced at calming Will down.

"Total honesty…do you think I'm in over my head? Am I a good enough parent?"

Lee shook off his post-coital fog and collected his thoughts.

"Will, you are not in over your head, you're an *exceptional* parent. Of course you're good enough. Your dad chose you for a reason, because there is no one else in this world who could do a better job of raising these kids—not Dave, and *certainly* not Eleanor." Lee knew the specter of his grandmother taking custody of her grandchildren and whisking them off to a privileged life in Atherton was a constant source of panic for Will.

There was a long pause at the other end of the phone. "You're *sure*?"

"I'm positive."

"Okay."

"Can I go back to my date now?"

"Yeah, I think I'm good for now. Is it the flight attendant or the Brazilian model?"

"The latter."

"Have fun."

"I am."

Will put down the phone and tried to go to sleep, but the specter of his grandmother haunted his dreams...

Eleanor Simpson Thompkins Ross was richer than God. That's what his father used to say whenever Will asked why his grandmother had such a big house. When he was a boy, Will didn't see this as a condemnation, although he was suspicious about the tone in his father's voice. For Will, there was nothing but a thrill of anticipation when his parents loaded the family into the old Volvo station wagon to drive to his grandmother's estate in Atherton. He itched at the chance to swim in the huge turquoise blue swimming pool or play tennis or volleyball on the soft lawn courts. There were enormous oak trees to climb, and a pond where he and Dave would sail wooden boats that they made by hand, pushing them with sticks across the glassy water as they ran around trying to catch them. It was an enchanted place, guarded by a huge iron gate with the word "Oakhaven" on it that would grind open slowly to let them through when his father announced who he was into a speaker box. Then they would drive down a long road of tall trees lined up like soldiers until they reached a vast circular driveway and an enormous three-story stone house surrounded by flowers and statues. It was bigger than any house Will had ever seen in Berkeley, in fact any house he had ever seen in his life.

Eleanor Simpson Thompkins Ross loved her grandchildren as much as she loved her son and his wife, and she indulged them in every way she could. There were horses to ride and water fountains to splash in and two giant staircases winding up from the living room they would slide down with pillowcases, racing to see who could get to the bottom first, their grandmother timing them with the giant French hall clock. There were picnics and elegant holiday dinners with candles and blue china and butlers in black suits serving endless rounds of food, more than anyone could eat, ending with colorful trays of sweet desserts and his mother playing their favorite Italian songs on her violin, the notes rising above them to the pastel angels painted on the ceiling, holding watch over them all. Years later, when Will was in medical school and Dan and Jules were born, the rituals began all over again, and the house, to his grandmother's delight, was filled once more with squealing children playing in the halls and the gardens.

Then there was silence.

The heartache of telling his grandmother that her only son had been killed was the hardest thing Will had ever done. He wanted to tell her in person, but with the distance to Atherton and two small children to care for, it wasn't practical. As practiced as he was as an ER doctor having to inform loved ones about the loss of their sons and daughters and brothers and fathers, he found himself mute when confronted with her innocent voice as she picked up the phone that awful morning, unaware of the arrow about to strike her. When he finally found the strength to speak, she responded with choked silence and then a wail of pain. "Both?" she cried out incredulously, "*both* of them...*gone*?"

He didn't blame his grandmother for wanting custody of Dan and Jules. They were the fresh green shoots out of her beloved son, all she had left of those all-too-brief halcyon days when everyone's world, at least everyone that mattered to her, was bright and full of happiness. But it was Will who won her prize.

"Take good care of my little loves," his mother said as she looked into Will's eyes and kissed him tenderly at the airport that fated day.

His father was more pragmatic. That morning, before they left for their flight, as his mother was giving instructions to Maria and kissing her children goodbye, Henry Thompkins sat his son down in his study to show him all the paperwork he would need in the event of their demise.

"It's all here," he pointed to the drawer in the old mahogany desk where Will had watched him read and study for as long as he could remember, "and it's filed with the lawyer. He'll take care of everything. The house and everything else is in a trust for all of you. You are to have guardianship of Dan and Jules, Will. Not your grandmother."

"Dad, nothing is going to happen to you—"

"It doesn't hurt to plan, son, so listen to what I'm saying. If anything happens to us, *you* have legal custody. We want them to live here in Berkeley, in *this* house. I love your grandmother, but never underestimate her. She can be formidable."

"Never underestimate her." The words bored their way into Will's consciousness. He and his grandmother were now engaged in an endless chess game in which he had to be wary of every maneuver—however innocent it might seem on the surface. Eleanor Simpson Thompkins Ross was very, very good at playing chess.

Will gave up on sleep and dropped his feet to the floor. He walked down the hallway to Danny's room, surprised to find him without his sister, who usually joined him some time in the middle of the night, a primal yearning to be close to her twin. The boy was deep in the blissful sleep of a 6-year old. Will curled in next to him, lying there for a long time listening to the soothing sound of his breathing. Before long, Jules wandered in, Malibu Barbie dangling at her side in carefree pink abandon.

"I had a bad dream, can I sleep here?"

"Sure, climb in."

"Did you have a bad dream too?"

"Kind of."

"Mommy says butterfly kisses make bad dreams go away. Here..." She put her face up close to his and fluttered her eyelashes against his cheek, the fragrance of her freshly shampooed hair wafting up to him.

"I think mommy's right."

"She gives them to me when I'm asleep."

"She does?"

"Yeah, that's why I usually have good dreams. She must have forgot tonight."

He stroked her hair. "She must have. Here, I'll give you one." He returned the kiss and she giggled. "How's that?"

"Good." She snuggled under the blankets, and the three of them fell into a blissful sleep.

The next morning Lee wandered through the back door of the Thompkins kitchen, as he did most mornings looking for coffee and food.

"Morning."

"Morning. Coffee is ready."

"Thanks."

"Thanks for talking me down last night."

"No problem." Lee grabbed a cup and leaned against the counter searching his friend's face. "So how are you? Did you get any sleep?"

"Yeah, finally. I slept in Danny's bed. Then Jules had a bad dream, so she came in with us."

"All three of you in that twin bed?"

"Yeah. It was a little crowded, but surprisingly tranquilizing—like having all your chicks in the nest."

"You're a psych dissertation waiting to be written, you know that?"

"Yeah, I know. Oatmeal?"

"Sure." Will dropped a wad of steaming oatmeal into a bowl and handed it to Lee.

"So how was the date?

"Okay."

"You're back on with Carlita?"

"We stay in touch."

"Is there something there, or is it just the sex?"

"No, it's pretty much just the sex."

"Hmm. Must be nice. I wouldn't know."

"I keep telling you, I can set you up. There are half a dozen women who would love to go out with you. You're a very attractive guy—in your own way."

"Gee, thanks mom."

"Women love men with kids, you know, it's wired into their DNA." Lee considered himself an expert on the psychology of women.

"Do I look like have room in my life for a relationship?"

"Who said anything about a relationship—I'm talking about sex. You need SEX." At that he saw Jules from the corner of his eye padding her way into the kitchen behind Will.

"...seven, eight, nine ten. And that's how you count to ten." Will looked at him incredulously.

"Wha...?" A second later Jules came into Will's view, Malibu Barbie still in tow. "Oh. Good morning baby."

"Morning. Are we counting? I can count to 1000."

"I know you can, I was just telling Will that."

Will smiled.

"I'm not giving up on persuading you about six, you know. It's a very important number."

"That it is." Will said wistfully. And he plopped a bowl of oatmeal on the table in front of Jules.

four

Will checked his image in the bathroom mirror one last time. He looked decent, but tired. Long days at the hospital, split shifts so he could be home for dinner, and scant hours of sleep were taking a toll. He patted on some aftershave and straightened the shirt Lee had picked out for him on a shopping excursion with the kids to make him more presentable for dating. He smiled at the recollection of the saleswoman at Nordstrom striking up a conversation with Danny and referring to Lee and him as 'your dads.' They had become so ridiculously domestic, shopping for kid's clothes and buying groceries together, everyone thought they were gay partners. Lee was right, it was time to date again. He desperately needed to remember what it was like to be normal. He needed *six*.

This date was a set-up with a flight attendant Lee knew who was in town on a layover. She shared an apartment in the

City with other FAs, and she came home regularly enough to call San Francisco home, which is how Lee knew her. Lee was a magnet for single women who eschewed attachment; Will was awed at how he managed to meet the dizzying array of casual sex partners that rotated through his life.

"Remember," Lee instructed, "take the intensity down a notch. Be cool. Don't think too much about it, just enjoy and follow her cue. Don't talk about your kids, this isn't an interview for a potential soulmate, it's just a date. And don't talk about your work, you're an ER doc, that's *way* too intense for most women. Keep it light." Will thought briefly that he should be embarrassed about how much instruction he needed in what used to come naturally, but he was way past that point. His personal life outside of the kids had been flatlined for so long, he needed help to resuscitate it.

He put on a sports jacket and headed out the door to the waterfront restaurant where they were going to meet. Halfway there his cell phone rang. He recognized Katrina's number. *She was cancelling.* Some excuse about an unexpected flight she had to take to Singapore, Milan, Paris, Cleveland, whatever. Or maybe she had a headache, food poisoning, a sick cat, a dead aunt. Let's face it, who would want to date him? He didn't travel or sail or play tennis or hang out in hip cocktail lounges. He lived in the house he grew up in with two little kids and his Latina housekeeper. He played pick-up basketball in the driveway with his best friend from high school.

Will resigned himself to rejection and picked up the phone—*she was running late!* Could he pick her up at her house so she didn't have to take a cab? *She wasn't cancelling!* He exhaled with relief. He was going on a *real* date. He felt the ripple of his old identity pass through him. He pulled the car up to Katrina's building on the Embarcadero. It was a rabbit warren of modern apartments wrapped along the waterfront facing the Bay Bridge and the Giants ballpark, the kind of place he thought Lee would live in before he opted for the domestic calm of his little bungalow on Avalon. He suddenly felt like he was a thousand miles from Berkeley, in some kind of alternate reality where beautiful people sat sipping martinis at sunset and went to art shows and jogged along the waterfront and had casual sex with other martini-drinking beautiful people. A world where there were no Malibu Barbie beach houses and plastic dinosaurs to bang into in the night, no mismatched shoes five minutes before school, no debates about how all the bath water wound up on the bathroom floor or who let the dog chew up the couch cushions.

He pulled into the space Katrina had instructed him to use, grabbed the wine from the front seat and went searching for her apartment number. It was dusk, and the lights along the waterfront and crowning the Bay Bridge were beginning to twinkle to life as the evening fog rolled in. The pungent smell of the bay was intoxicating. How long had it been since he'd been in the City in the evening? He couldn't remember. It seemed like a lifetime ago. He felt invigorated as the soft damp of the San Francisco fog enveloped him. Lee was right: he *needed* this. He vowed he would get out more. Maybe he would bring Danny and Jules to a ballgame, a night game, so they could see all the lights—no, too cold for them, a day game maybe. They could get hotdogs and those big foam fingers, and they could take Maria, she loved baseball, she had baseball cards of all her favorite Latin players stuck into the mirror above her dresser...

He reeled himself back in and concentrated on the task at hand. *He was on a date.* He straightened his shirt one last time, ran his hand through his hair and pushed the doorbell. He shouldn't have been surprised when he saw Katrina in the doorway, Lee had impeccable taste in women, but she was *beautiful*. Long dark hair, blue eyes, and a lovely athletic body that moved gracefully. She was relaxed and confident. She took the wine from his hand and welcomed him into the living room while she retrieved two glasses and a wine opener. The room was small, but arranged around a large bay window revealing a glistening view of the waterfront.

"This is a great apartment."

"Yeah, it's nice, isn't it? Not as much fun when all 5 of us are here," she laughed.

She had a luminous smile, Will thought. She popped open the wine bottle with ease and poured two generous glasses. "Here's to blind dates."

"To blind dates," Will smiled and clinked his glass to hers, feeling more like his old self by the minute.

By the time they got back from the restaurant, he was two more glasses of wine in and had fallen hard. She was funny, telling hilarious stories about what it was like to travel the world as a flying cocktail waitress, and *smart*. She had graduated from the Rhode Island School of Design and worked for a prestigious New York firm before deciding that 16-hour days answering to the needs of clients were not for her. She'd lived in Bali, London, Florence and Amsterdam, moving whenever a slot came open that interested her. In short, she lived the exact opposite life that Will had lived.

He couldn't remember a time when he hadn't been laser-focused on his goal of becoming a doctor—graduating at 17 from high school, 21 from Berkeley and then onto med school, his internship, residency, and ER fellowship all in commando mode, never veering from trajectory. He spent his free time doing volunteer work for vaccination clinics in Mexico and disaster sites for Doctors Without Borders. He rarely traveled for pleasure, except for the summers he was conscripted abroad with his parents when he would chafe at the time lost from studying while they dragged him to museums and concerts and sidewalk cafes. It rattled his sensibilities that they could sit for hours visiting with their friends, conversing lazily over wine and long meals, chatting with passersby and watching life unfold in the street as if there was no urgency at all. God, what he would give to have those hours back with them now. How *narrow* his life had become.

Katrina was the antithesis of him. She lived easily in the wide world, with no plan and no ties. It was intoxicating. He was so locked up, so scarred over from the events of the last few years. She was relaxed—supple and serene, with a casual sexuality. When she invited him back into the house after dinner he was full of lust for her—for her bohemian life, her freedom, her body. He wanted to breathe her in to make himself whole again.

She walked over to turn on the music and a blues piano began to play seductively through the apartment. He was trying to keep his composure, but the wine was making it difficult. She was dressed in a paper-light silk dress—was it Balinese?—that wrapped gently around the curves of her body with a tie, falling open slightly at her breasts and thighs. She never adjusted it, she hardly seemed to notice when it shifted or fell open as she moved gracefully across the room—or maybe she was seducing him. He didn't know anymore, his instincts were blunted from disuse and from the wine. He only knew he wanted her badly. He wanted to pull that tie and open the floodgates to her body, to his own body.

She curled up next to him on the couch and ran her fingers through her long hair, pushing it away from her face. He reached over and cupped his hand under her chin, then succumbed to the urge and leaned in to kiss her. She responded, biting his lower lip gently and pulling her body up to his so she was pressed against him. He could feel her warm breath on his neck and feel her heartbeat. Now they were all mouths and fingers. He pushed the silk dress open and his hands gathered up her bare breasts as he pressed his lips against them hungrily. She responded, arching her back to give her body to him, the dress now fallen open revealing her lovely thighs. She was naked underneath it! He pulled the tie and ran his lips across the length of her lithe body, kissing her breasts and running his mouth down her abdomen. She raised her hips up to meet his lips and he lost himself in her bliss, pulling off his clothes frantically so he could lay his naked body onto her warm skin. At every point their bodies touched, his own skin lit up on fire—he was *starved* for the touch of a woman. They moved to her bed and made love into the night, until he was so spent he could only lie in the softness of her sheets and stare up at her longingly as she lay on top of him with her legs wrapped around his body, her long brown hair spread across his chest.

When he woke in the morning she was gone. He vaguely recalled her kissing him goodbye, but he had slept so deeply and blissfully he couldn't remember if he responded. He shuffled into the kitchen and found coffee waiting, along with a note thanking him for a great night. She was off to Hong Kong. She would let him know when she was back in the city again. It was a kind note, but clearly offered no commitment for the future. *He was a one-night stand.* He poured some coffee and sat on the sofa taking in the morning view of the San Francisco Bay. The fog was beginning to roll back across the water revealing the masts of early morning sailboats headed for Sausalito and Tiburon. Later commuter ferries and tourist boats would scatter across the bay, and the crowds would fill the waterfront making their way to the ballpark for the game, but for now the city was not quite awake, and it was peaceful. It was the kind of peace he didn't often get living with two small children. He took a sip of coffee and smiled at the recollection of the previous night. He was a one-night stand, but *oh, what a night.* He felt alive again.

five

Will checked his watched nervously and yelled up the stairs. It seemed to him now that he spent half his waking hours trying to round up children for one reason or another. Breakfast, school, play dates, music lessons, doctors appointments, dinner, bedtime. It was a never-ending job. "Everybody down here RIGHT NOW, we've got to go!" He turned to Lee, who was sitting on the couch working on his laptop. "Did you check the weather again? Are they still predicting rain?" He peered over Lee's shoulder to look at the computer screen. Lee slapped the laptop closed.

"It's fine. It may rain on them a day or two, but they have a tent and rain gear. They're *camping*, that's what's camping is all about."

"I know but they just got over bad colds, I don't want them sleeping in a damp tent all week."

It's July, they'll be fine. Stop stressing. They're seven years old, they can handle it, they had a great time last year. They're excited, don't ruin it for them with your paranoia."

"What's that supposed to mean…?" Will looked offended. "DANIEL AND JULIANA GET DOWN HERE RIGHT NOW!" He turned back to Lee. "Being a safe parent does not constitute paranoia."

Both children presented themselves in front of Will, familiar with the drill. "Okay, before we go, let's go over the rules one more time." Lee rolled his eyes.

"*Again?*" This time it was Danny.

"Yes, *again*. It never hurts to remind ourselves about safety. You can't be *too* safe. Ready?"

Like a Greek chorus, they took turns reciting the checklist of potential threats:

"Never go near the water without a grownup, you can drown."

"Wear sunscreen every day so you don't get cancer."

"Stay away from deer, they bite—even though they're pretty."

"Always bring a sweater or jacket in case it gets cold, even if you're hot."

"Never go walking anywhere without a grownup."

"If you get lost, stay in one place."

"No food in the tent, cause the bears might eat you."

"That's good!" Will looked satisfied. "Anything else?" They struggled to recall any forgotten rules.

"Check for ticks--EVERY night." Will prompted. "That's *very* important. And don't touch any leaves or bushes that might be poison oak. Do you have your poison oak pictures?" They nodded. "And how about your pictures of ticks?

"Yeah, in my bag." Danny said, patting his knapsack.

"They're gross Will!" Juliana made a face.

"They *are* gross. They're even grosser if they get on your skin, because they can give you disease. So you have to check carefully for 'em every night. And what about the campfire?"

"Don't sit too close to it, 'cause sparks can fly and get on your clothes and start you on fire."

"Right." Will looked pleased with himself. Lee was leaning his forehead into his hands.

"And last, but not least, always put on mosquito repellant, every single morning, so the mosquitos don't bite you..." At that, he began to pinch both of them until they were squealing and giggling. "Okay, now you're ready to go camping. It's going to be great! Grab your gear, gotta pull your own weight." Lee laughed at the concept.

"Will, are you going to drive up and sleep in the tent with us again?" Jules asked as the car wound through the twisted back roads of the Santa Cruz mountains. Will gave a sidelong glance at Lee.

"No, baby, not this time."

"Why?"

"Because you guys are old enough to be up there by yourselves now, and I know you're going to do great."

"Yeah, *they'll* be fine." Lee said sarcastically.

As they entered the camp Will felt the familiar anxiety creep into his throat. It was bucolic, a charming throwback to another era, with log cabins set among the redwoods and sequoias, a giant stone campfire pit surrounded by benches for nightly bonfires, and a circle of pup tents, each assigned to various campers, with two large counselor's tents in the center to keep an eye on things. It was filled with the fragrant smell of green needles and soil warmed by the sun. It was also, and this was the reason Will chose it, surrounded by high cyclone fencing and locked gates, as safe as any faux wilderness experience could be. In spite of it all, the idea of Dan and Jules being physically out of his reach was viscerally painful to Will. As they walked down the path to their assigned tent he faked enthusiasm, but he was beginning to feel sick. In the ER he was a commando, navigating his world of blood and pain with a cool and steady hand. He could put his hands wrist-deep in the body of a car accident victim, wrestle down a crazed addict, be splattered with blood from a gunshot wound without flinching. But the idea of being out of immediate reach of his children filled him with cold panic. Once, when he had put them on a plane with Dave to spend time in Boston, he stood paralyzed in the airport parking lot watching the plane ascend into the clouds, his arms involuntarily lifted skyward, as if he needed to hold them all up out of harm's way by himself.

"Wow, it's way cool, right guys!" Lee was trying to distract them from tapping into Will's anxiety. Will crawled inside the tent with them to check it out, pulling on the stakes, checking for ticks, viewing the line of sight to the counselor's tent, which, at his request, was directly across from theirs. "Everything okay then?" Lee prodded, "No bugs, no poison ivy, no small animals lurking about waiting to attack them?"

Will sneered at him.

"All the other parents have left. You've interrogated the counselors and inspected their tent...are you ready to actually let them *camp*?"

Will steeled himself to the prospect of leaving and put his arms around them both. "Okay, give me kisses, its time for Lee and me to go." Jules hugged him hard and then bounced away.

"We're going to a marshmallow bake!"

"That's wonderful, baby, go have fun." She stopped short and looked into his eyes.

"Are you going to be okay without us, Will?" Will looked away. He knew she could read him; she was deeply intuitive, just like his mother. He kissed her again.

"I'm going to be *great*, don't worry."

"We'll be careful about the fire." Danny assured him.

"Good boy." Will smiled. "Now go roast some marshmallows." He kissed them both one last time, feeling their soft cheeks against his face, breathing in the scent of their skin before he watched them scamper away to join the other children.

"Okay, let's go."

"You okay?"

"Yeah."

"This is good for them, you know."

"I know."

There was a long silence between them.

"I *hate* them being away from me. I can't help it, it's like someone sawed off a limb… I'm such a fucking control freak."

"I know, but you've got to do it, buddy. For them *and* for you. It's time for you to have a life."

"I know…why can't I seem to do that?"

"I don't know, it's the way you're wired. You're a commando doctor and a commando parent—it's how you take on the world. You just need to put some of that energy into finding a relationship. You need a woman. It's been three years since your parents died, it's time to start having a normal life again."

"What's normal? I don't even know anymore."

"It's time to find out, and this is a good time to start. The kids are at camp, Maria's with her sister, you've got a whole week to yourself with no one to worry about but you. Why don't you ask out that gorgeous attorney who was hitting on you at the fundraiser?"

"The one with the black leather skirt?"

"Yeah. She was perfect for you, just what you need."

"I don't know if I'm ready for that kind of commitment."

"It's just a date! When's the last time you actually went on a date with a woman?"

Will thought back to his liaisons with Katrina. It had been over a year since she moved to Singapore, and he still missed her. She was the only woman who knew how to quell the bottomless pain that haunted him. He loved knowing she would breeze in on a random night and call him up to come over, and they would talk and make love in the soft sheets of her bed until dawn, until she would have to fly off again leaving him with a last kiss. He knew he never possessed her, but now she was really gone. Late night phone calls slipped into emails and then emails began to go unanswered. She had moved on. It's what she knew how to do best.

"I don't know. A couple of months ago, I guess. I tried to date Linda. She wouldn't go out with me."

"You do not want to date your kids' pediatrician. That's a commitment. Linda's smart, she knows that's an accident waiting to happen. What did she tell you?"

"She said she liked my kids too much to date me. Apparently I have a reputation as a commitment-phobic guy."

"You *are* a commitment phobic guy."

"Look who's talking. You call Carlita a commitment?"

"I learned Spanish to date her."

"Yeah, so you could tell her what kind of sex you liked." They both laughed as the car swung away from the camp, back down the winding roads of the Santa Cruz mountains into the buzz of the Santa Clara valley. "I miss my kids already," Will grimaced, as Lee braced himself for a long week.

"Can you meet for lunch?"

"It depends. Did you call her?"

"Yes, I called her. "

"When are you going out?"

"Tomorrow night."

"Good. Still coming Thursday for poker?"

"Yeah."

"We'll expect a full report."

"Very classy. Go on a date and report the details to my poker buddies, I'm sure she'd appreciate that."

"Trust me, she'll be reporting everything to her lawyer girlfriends. So you better perform."

"Thanks for the pressure.

"I'm just saying. She's a high-powered attorney, you're in the big leagues now. You're going to have to step up your game. Where are you taking her?"

"Chez Panisse"

"Berkeley?" He sounded annoyed. "Why not Slanted Door?"

"Slanted Door is...you know...where I used to go with Katrina."

"You've got to get past Katrina, buddy, she's gone."

"I know, I just...I'm not ready to go back there."

"Okay, Chez Panisse is a little too "Berkeley" for her if you ask me, but I guess it'll do."

"What are you planning to wear?"

"Listen, I've got patients lined up..."

"It has to be the black shirt."

"Can we discuss my wardrobe later, when I don't have patients bleeding in my waiting room?"

"Okay, I'll see you at noon."

Will clicked off the phone and felt the old dread fill him. He didn't want to go on this date. He would be much happier camping with his kids. He missed them horribly, he lived with a perpetual knot in his gut imagining all the things that could happen to them. What was worse, he hated the house when they were away. It was eerily quiet—no one running to the door to greet him when he came home at night, no smells of dinner cooking or the chattering away of Maria telling him about their day, no squeal of noisy children playing. The emptiness just made him think of his parents and the void left by their absence.

It was as if the house got bigger and colder. He just wanted the week to be over and for all of them to be sitting around the old redwood table together in the kitchen, safe and sound.

Now he was going to *have* to go through with the date, there would be no peace with Lee if he didn't, and this woman did not seem like the type to take a late cancellation lightly. He just had to steel himself to it.

He sat across from Lee in the hospital cafeteria picking at his lunch. "So listen, I've called the camp three times this morning and no one is answering. Doesn't that seem weird to you?"

"They've probably got you on caller ID."

"It doesn't make sense, what if there was an emergency?"

"Did it occur to you they might be out *camping*? That is the point of being up there you know."

"It's common courtesy, if a parent calls to check in, someone should be there to answer the phone."

"Okay, let's talk about your date."

"I'd rather not."

"I know, but it's important. You've been tanking lately on your personal life and you've got to go through with this. I'm sensing you're thinking of bailing."

"I'm not thinking of bailing." *How did he know these things?*

"Good, because it's important to get back on the horse, you know?"

"I know." He stared at his half eaten sandwich, which no longer looked appealing.

"I've done a little intelligence and I think she could be good for you. She's smart, tough, accomplished. Apparently she has a good sense of humor."

"*Apparently*? What does that mean?"

"Just, be positive, okay?"

"I'm being positive."

"You can talk about your work, she'll get that, but not the kids too much. She's not really the domestic type."

"Got it."

"And wear the black shirt."

"I'm *going* to wear the black shirt."

"I can't convince you about the Slanted Door? I've got connections there, I can still get you a reservation."

"I'm going to Chez Panisse."

"Okay, I'm done then. Are you going to eat those fries?"

"I'm not hungry, take 'em. Although they're not exactly what you need with your high blood pressure."

"My high blood pressure is not what's going to kill me. What's going to kill me is trying to jump-start your personal life."

seven

Miranda Holloway was a high-powered attorney at a prestigious law firm in San Francisco. That was about all Will knew about her. He was introduced to her at a charity auction for the hospital and they struck up a conversation about how tedious but necessary charity auctions were. What Will remembered most was that she was wearing sky high black stiletto heels and a black leather skirt that was slit up the side, so when she moved you could see the full length of her well-toned leg. He remembered wondering briefly if she wore it in court, strategically revealing the slit at opportune moments as part of her litigating technique. She was definitely stunning. Her blond hair was pulled back tight in a ponytail and she was wearing blood red nail polish that looked just a little intimidating. He thought it was calculated to look that way, because every time she gestured with her hand it seemed to emphasize to him that she meant business.

He didn't really think she was his type, but frankly he no longer knew what his type was. Yes, he did—Katrina. Funny, carefree, sexy Katrina. He wished it was her he was driving to meet. She wouldn't care about his black shirt or at what restaurant they ate, she would welcome him with her body and make him feel whole again.

He arrived at Chez Panisse a little early and walked up the stairs to find its owner, Alice Waters, greeting guests. She hugged him warmly and asked how he was doing. His parents had been close friends with Alice, and he always felt comfortable in her restaurant. He had so many happy memories of family dinners inside the warm wood walls that held the fragrant smells of many years of cooking from the open kitchen. He was hoping that bringing Miranda there would give him an emotional advantage.

Alice sat him in his favorite booth and brought him a glass of wine, which he downed nervously as he waited. Miranda appeared at the top of the stairs, precisely on time, in a tight red sleeveless dress and matching red heels and lipstick, blonde ponytail flying. She looked like an alien from another planet as she strutted through the tables filled with earth toned, sensibly dressed Berkeleyans, her stilettos clicking on the worn oak floor. All eyes turned to look at the two of them as she greeted Will. Lee was right—the restaurant *was* too small for her.

"Can I get you some wine?"

"It's been a brutal day, I'd love a martini." she flung her enormous purse into the booth and scanned the wooden walls and Arts and Craft decor. "Do they *have* them here?"

What was he thinking--of course she was a martini kind of woman. He called over the server.

Miranda ordered without pleasantries. "Martini. 209 gin, very dry, with a twist, stirred. Please." She looked through the server as if she was transparent.

"So, tough day?" It seemed like the only entry point Will could find for conversation.

"You wouldn't believe it." She rolled her eyes and took a sip of water. "First my idiot secretary corrupted the file he was supposed to email to me, and then after I finally got a copy of it to review, I careened through the city to my two o'clock only to find out the other attorney called a postponement due to 'illness in the family.' It was a nightmare." She glanced over Will's shoulder to see if her martini was being made yet. "How about you? You work in an ER, that must be a tough job." She said it with a slight thrill in her voice, as if it was a badge of honor.

Will thought about his day. A drugged up stabbing victim, a forty-year old stroke patient with a severe brain bleed that probably meant she would never be whole again, and an 11-year old in a car accident who they lost on the operating table. All of them with family who had to be told the news. He didn't want to share any of it with Miranda Holloway. "It can be a tough job."

The martini came in the nick of time, and she used the opportunity to toast, "To tough jobs."

"To tough jobs," he said, clinking glasses with her. He thought longingly of his children nestled by the campfire roasting marshmallows. He imagined driving up and surprising them, feeling their arms wrapped around him and settling down together for the night in the tent where he could hear the soft sound of their breathing.

"So three hours later my client was six million dollars richer and we were cracking open champagne on his ex-wife's yacht while she was still walking down the dock." Miranda was laughing out loud, her head thrown back, ponytail swaying. Will didn't know if it was the second glass of wine or total resignation, but she was growing on him. It was refreshing how completely self-possessed she was. She was downright ballsy. Before he knew it more than two hours had passed. He was taking care of the check when she leaned in close to him, putting her hand on his knee under the table.

"Shall we go back to your place?" He was taken aback, but ready for game.

"That sounds great." He smiled and put his hand on top of hers under the table.

"Why don't we leave my car here, I can pick it up later."

"Let's do that," he said, wondering if he was really up to what was in store.

He turned the key on the front door of the house and escorted her through. In the hallway she kicked off her heels. She seemed less intimidating without them, more life size. She untied her ponytail, her blond hair falling down around her shoulders, and began to kiss him long and hard, locking her hands behind him and pressing him up against her body. *Okay, things were going to escalate fast.* He threw the car keys onto a nearby table and returned the kiss, his hands caressing the length of her body, feeling her curves beneath the red dress. Now he was crazy with desire for her. She reached down to unbuckle his belt and slip her hand down into his groin, releasing him. Her mouth was all over him. He unzipped her dress and it dropped to the ground, revealing tantalizing red lace underwear. *She was gorgeous!* Her breasts were firm, her body tan and toned. And she was strong. She pulled off the rest of his clothes as they made their way to the couch. He was on fire with raw lust, kneading her breasts, tearing the lace underwear as he pulled it off of her, grabbing at her body madly. She made love to him fiercely, biting and clenching and pounding into him until they climaxed wildly. He didn't know how much time had passed—minutes? An hour? She grabbed his wrists and pulled him playfully upstairs, both of them naked, picking up her shoes along the way, searching for his bed. She headed down the hall looking for the master bedroom, but he still wasn't ready for that, so he veered her into the guestroom, where she started seducing him all over again, teasing him, posed on the edge of the bed wearing nothing but the red stillettos. They made love two or three times more, he couldn't remember, he was lost in a fog of sex and satiation. He had never been with a woman like her.

In the morning he woke to find her asleep across from him in the bed, curled on a pillow, blond hair wrapped in a knot behind her. She looked tender, less fierce than she did when she was awake. He went downstairs to make coffee. He wanted to sit for a few minutes at the kitchen table to sort out his thoughts, but he didn't want her to think he was the kind of guy to disappear when morning came, so instead he brought two cups up to the bedroom.

"Morning." He saw her stir and handed her a cup.

"Thank you." She said smiling.

"For the coffee or last night?" He smiled back at her. She was beautiful lying there in the bed.

"Both." She sat up, wrapped in the sheets, holding the cup in both hands.

"I don't usually do that," she laughed. It was more a statement of fact than any suggestion of remorse.

"Neither do I." He said, sitting next to her on the edge of the bed. He leaned over and kissed her forehead.

"You just looked so…"

"Needy?" Will laughed.

"No, attractive."

"You're pretty attractive yourself." He smiled at the understatement. "Sorry about the lingerie."

"That's what it's meant for." She glanced at her phone on the nightstand. "Eight o'clock, I'm going to have to go soon. I have a ten o'clock in the city. "

"Can I get you some breakfast?"

"Eggs and toast would be great." She was used to asking for what she wanted.

"Eggs and toast it is."

"You cook, I'll shower." She got out of bed and walked naked to the bathroom with no self-consciousness. Her body in the morning light was even more spectacular, clearly the result of many hours at the gym. In spite of the allure, he suddenly felt exhausted. He was secretly glad she had to leave; he wasn't sure what to make of their night together. He needed time to himself.

He went downstairs to make breakfast, and in twenty minutes or so she appeared, dressed smartly in a fresh black sheath dress and stilettos, ponytail in place, ready to take on the next litigation. He raised his eyebrows when he saw her and smiled. "Did you have that delivered?"

"Big purse." She smiled back. He poured himself more coffee and put the eggs and toast on the table in front of her.

"So you have kids?" He almost choked on his coffee.

"I do. Although, I don't usually talk about them on a first date."

"It's okay, the Tyrannosaurus poking me in the back on the couch was my first clue."

"Ah. Sorry about that. I thought I got them all." He smiled.

"I saw their rooms. Boy and girl?"

He nodded. "Twins. They just turned seven. They're my siblings. Long story."

"You're an interesting man."

"If by that you mean I have baggage, you're right. Quite a lot, actually."

"I'm okay with baggage. I don't do well with kids."

"That's ironic, I don't do well without them."

"Where are they?"

"At summer camp."

"How long?"

"Till Sunday."

"So…see you Friday?"

Will was taken aback. "I'd like that."

"Good." She smiled and dove into her eggs with gusto.

eight

Thursday night poker at Lee's had been a tradition since med school. Players came and went, but the core group remained the same. Lee, Will, Mike Frasier, an orthopedic surgeon married with two kids, and Seth Elliott, a cardiologist who was single. Sometimes Dave joined them when he was in town from Boston, but these days it was usually just the four of them, poring over the week's events—work and domestic. For Will, Thursday night was his only regular indulgence away from the kids and he usually looked forward to it, but tonight he knew he was going to be grilled on his latest dating foray. His personal life had become so pathetic, they felt compelled to cheerlead him on. It was humiliating. He walked into the Lee's living room to find them all sitting at the poker table with expectant looks on their faces.

"Well?

"Did you go?"

"Yes, I went." They hooted and applauded. He found himself smiling—he felt like he was in high school again. "It was just a date, okay, it was no big deal. We went to dinner."

"Are you kidding, I saw her at the auction, she was fucking gorgeous." Mike said. "Did she wear that black leather skirt?"

"She wore a red dress, that is all I'm going to say. A little decorum please."

"She spent the night," Lee said. Now they were whistling and catcalling.

"Jesus, how do you know that—are you stalking me?"

"I live three doors away, I was getting my newspaper when you walked out this morning."

"Fine, she spent the night. That's the last thing I'm saying on the subject."

"Good for you," Seth said, with his cardiologist's sensibility. "I respect you for being a gentleman."

"Oh bullshit," Mike said, "I go to bed every night with the same woman, I want details. Was she as good in bed as she looked?" The cowboy surgeon, had no such sensibilities.

Will smiled and shook his head. "I am not going there, so don't even try."

"Here, have a shooter" Lee put a shot of tequila and a beer in front of Will.

"Since when are we drinking tequila shooters at poker night?"

"It's a special occasion."

"Uh huh. I'll stick to beer, thank you. I have to work in the morning."

"Oh come on, just one. To celebrate you jump-starting your dating life." They all raised their shot glasses to toast him.

"Oh, what the hell." Will downed the tequila. "Just *one.*" The rest of them took their shots and Lee dealt the cards. Four shooters and a few hours later Will's head was spinning and he was spilling information like a teenager.

"She was fucking *amaz-ing*! I've never had sex with a woman like that, she was fearless! She does this one thing with her teeth that....I don't know, I don't even know how she did it."

"More details," Mike demanded.

"Nah, I've said way too much already. I've gotta go before you twist anything else out of me."

"You're going to leave us hanging?"

"Okay, Seth said, "let's not take advantage of him, he's going to be hurting enough in the morning."

"Just give me something to look forward to," Mike prodded some more, "are you going to see her again?"

"My kids are coming home Sunday you know."

"All the more reason."

"If you must know, we're going out tomorrow night." More applause from the group.

"That's good enough for me--I'll let my imagination do the rest. You can give us a report next week. I'll bring the tequila." Mike was laughing hard.

Will walked home with his head pounding. He was glad it was only a short distance to his door, because he was not in any shape to navigate. He walked through the big empty house to his bedroom, pulled off his clothes and dropped onto the bed. He didn't know if it was the tequila or his imagination, but he fell asleep to the tantalizing smell of sex and perfume.

When he woke up the next morning his mind and body were in pain. He remembered why he didn't drink tequila. Worse, he now had second and third thoughts about meeting Miranda again that night. What was he thinking accepting a second date? It was his penis talking! The relationship had nowhere to go. She was *way* out of his league, she lived in a world that was stratospheres above him, and even worse, she didn't like kids, and he had two of them. *He was flying too close to the sun!* Damn Lee for insisting he go out with her. He would have been perfectly happy to spend the night in a tent with his kids. Now he was committed to seeing her again. What could they possibly talk about? What could they possibly do that they hadn't already done—*several times over.*" He was miserable. He showered with his head still banging and headed to work, his refuge. As soon as he walked into his office he was confronted by Carlotta, his assistant.

"Rough night?"

"What was your first clue?"

"You look like hell."

"Good, I feel like hell too. You can thank Lee and his invitation to Jose Cuervo to join poker night."

"You're supposed to meet with Rob in half an hour."

"Perfect." Rob Weinberg was the Chief of Emergency Medicine at Mercy Hospital. He was Will's strongest supporter, promoting him early on to be his second in command and relying on him for help with hospital business. Will's head was full of slush, the thought of strategizing for an upcoming board review filled him with existential nausea.

"Can you cancel?" He was actually whining.

"I can try." Will trusted Carlotta with everything, she was the best nurse he'd ever worked with—whip-smart, tough and fast, but also tender with patients and their families which impressed him even more. She was his sounding board for all things professional and domestic—advice about his career, his children, and his personal life.

"So how did the date go?"

"Oh god, you too?"

"Look at me." She peered into his eyes. "You had *sex!*"

"It's been three days, how do you know that?"

"I'm a nurse. You had sex with that woman on the first date?"

"It's complicated."

"No it's not."

"Well *she's* complicated. I don't know, it just happened."

"Your house or hers?"

"Mine."

"In your *house*? Does she know you have children, because she did *not* look like the motherly type."

"She knows. What's worse, as long as you're judging, I'm going out with her again tonight, and I'm not happy about it, so you can enjoy my misery."

"Your children are coming home on Sunday."

"I'm aware of that. I don't intend to have sex for two days straight. Can we discuss work now?"

"Your house or hers tonight?"

"Hers...*the patients*?"

"Where does she live?"

"San Francisco...*the PATIENTS*?"

"Gall bladder in two, broken leg in four and a concussion in five. The residents have them handled."

"Thank you." The rest of the morning was a blur to him. All he could think about was how much he didn't want to go on the date with Miranda.

"Suck it up. You're overthinking this, it's just a date." Lee lectured him as they ate lunch. "She's not interested in a long term relationship, she's interested in sex, so enjoy it, it doesn't happen that often, especially to you."

"I'm telling you I'm in over my head. I have no idea what to do with this woman, she's...I don't know...*fierce*. I don't really *do* fierce."

"You must've done something right, she asked you on another date."

"It's pointless discussing this with you."

"What time are we picking up the kids on Sunday?"

"We're supposed to be there by noon, so we'll have to leave by 10:00 to be safe."

"Will your date be finished in time?" Lee laughed.

"Very funny, have you been talking to Carlotta?"

"Have fun tonight. I'll get the details on the ride up to camp Sunday. Are you going to eat the other half of that sandwich?"

"Take it. I can't eat."

nine

Will drove into San Francisco with a knot in his stomach. He was meeting Miranda at her apartment in The Rincon Towers, a pair of luxury glass and steel high-rises perched at the top of Rincon Hill near the waterfront. As he drove the car nearer, the building seemed to grow taller, rising up like a glass monolith, with the nearby buildings crouched down below it in supplication. He pulled up to the circular driveway and a valet met him, taking the car from him to park it. Another doorman held open the door and walked him through the ultra-modern glass-enclosed lobby to the elevator. *Ms. Holloway was expecting him.*

The doorman put his key into a special lock on the elevator to send him to the 60th floor, the penthouse. As the elevator began to rise, Will thought briefly how much his father would have chafed at such gratuitous luxury, but he was too stressed-out to deal with the guilt. He brought an expensive bottle of

Pinot Noir, which he tucked under his arm. He had debated bringing flowers too, but decided he would look too needy. He thought of her like a beautiful bird of prey, just waiting for her target to show signs of weakness so she could move in for the kill.

The elevator opened and he found himself standing in her marble entryway, awestruck. Across the room a 180 degree view of the city glimmered like a diamond tiara. *Wow.* He was accustomed to his grandmother's old-money, Atherton kind of wealth, but this was something else altogether. The apartment was an ultra modern cathedral of glass, with floor to ceiling curved windows that took full advantage of the view; all of San Francisco was laid out below them like a supper waiting to be devoured. It was pure Miranda—luxurious, stunning, modern, a little cold. There was a telescope in one window, and an imposing stone sculpture of something undecipherable dominating another. He recognized a pair of Mies van der Rohe chairs at one end of the room, and a long, black leather couch with chrome arms and legs at the other. In between, a huge white downy rug dominated the floor, held down by an amoeba-shaped glass Noguchi coffee table. Will imagined the room littered with Legos, baseball cards, Barbie dreamhouses and dog toys and laughed to himself. This was an alternate universe.

Miranda appeared in the hallway dressed in jeans and a ruby silk blouse that draped seductively over her breasts. She was barefoot, and she greeted him with a kiss that was surprisingly gentle.

"Come in." He handed her the wine. She seemed so pleased, he wished he had bought the flowers too. *She was maddeningly enigmatic.* "It's a beautiful night, I thought we could have dinner here." she said, linking his arm and leading him into an adjoining dining room, where an ebony black table and chairs was set with candles, white porcelain dishes and red cloth napkins. A single white iris rested in a tall crystal vase in the middle of the table.

"It's a fantastic apartment, Miranda, have you lived here long?"

"A year. I bought it after I made partner. It suits me...don't you think?" She poured the wine into two glasses. *Was that a hint of insecurity or was she being coy?*

"It suits you perfectly." He said. "It's beautiful." She smiled and led him back into the living room to sit on the couch. It was one of those couches designed more as an aesthetic statement than a place to sit. The back was low and slanted in such a way that you couldn't really recline very comfortably without your neck snapping back in an awkward pose. He wondered if that's what she liked about it, keeping people slightly off balance. She, on the other hand, was draped across it sinuously with no awkwardness at all, one arm languidly resting on the back and the other holding her glass of wine, her knees curled up under her, her bare feet peeking out with their blood red nail polish. Despite his warning to himself to not let the night spiral out of control, he was once again being pulled into her orbit by ever tightening gravitational circles. She was talking about some legal case he didn't understand, and each time she gestured, the glow of the candles reflected off her body seductively, revealing the curve of her breasts under the silk blouse.

They talked work and politics, always keeping it lofty, never a mention of his kids or her family. *Did she have a family, or was she sprung fully formed from Zeus's head?* As he listened to her talk he got tantalizing glimpses of softness underneath all that self-assurance, but she was not about to reveal it. Dinner was elegant, perched on the lip of the glass cathedral looking out over the city. It was a clear night and they could see out to the Golden Gate Bridge and across the bay to Berkeley and Oakland. It was a heady feeling living in the clouds.

They wandered back into the living room after dinner with glasses of 100-year-old port. It rolled across his tongue sweet and strong, blurring out the hard edges of his day. She looked incredibly appealing in her jeans and bare feet, all the fierceness put to rest for the night. He was so hungry for a woman's touch, he wanted desperately to make love to her again, to press his hands against those silky breasts and feel her legs wrapped around him tight and naked. Was she purposely asking him to make the first move this time? Was it calculated? He didn't really care. He reached over and kissed her, holding her face in both hands tenderly, tracing the line along her neck and earlobe with his lips. Her body gave into him, and before he knew it they were wrapped around each other, her breasts in his mouth, his hands caressing her, sliding off her jeans to reveal her beautiful body, her legs parted, her abdomen pressed up against him waiting to take him in. They lay on the downy fur of the white rug, rolling back and forth finding new ways to satisfy each other, using their lips and hands to tantalize each other's bodies. She was pure sexuality without inhibition. Her body was protean, yielding to him in every way he wanted to have her, and he wanted her over and over again. He didn't want the night to end—the softness of the white rug against him, her skin, her lips, her breasts, the warmth of her body as she took him inside her. The bliss of release. If only it didn't have to end.

They woke the next morning, still curled up together on the white rug, a soft blanket had somehow gotten wrapped over their naked bodies. The sun was rising, and light began to fill the apartment. He kissed her and stroked her body one more time before he got up and dressed. They made small talk over breakfast, but as the morning light filled the room a veil of melancholy settled over them. There was nowhere for the relationship to go. They both knew it. She would never embrace the complications of his life and kids, and he could never survive in this glass neverland of valets and private elevators and high-powered careers. He was too much Henry Thompkins' boy. He was an ER doctor, a fourth generation Berkeleyan with a messy life and two kids he loved more than he loved himself. It was time to go home.

ten

"The recital's in three hours and I'm a little worried about Jules' dress." Will was pacing across the living room. Lee was slouched on the couch watching college basketball with Jules, coaching her on the nuances of the game.

"I thought Maria made her one."

"She did, but you know, there are…cultural differences, I'm not sure it's going to work."

"What do you mean?"

"Well it's a little…over-the-top for a recital."

"She's eight. This is Berkeley. We're the epicenter of cultural diversity. How bad could it be? Let's see it."

"Baby, go and put on the recital dress Maria made you."

"Okay!" Juliana ran up the stairs to change and came down a few minutes later presenting herself proudly in front of Lee and Will. The dress was an inflated concoction of tulle, lace and glitter, with enormous puffed sleeves and rows of ruffles from top to bottom that swallowed her tiny frame in a sea of glistening black. The excess glitter wafted into the air as she moved. Lee's eyes widened as he put his hand over his mouth to stifle a laugh.

"Maria says I look like a fairy princess in it."

"You do, babe. You definitely do. It's…WOW. Like a princess…or *something*." He was working hard now to keep from bursting out laughing.

"You look beautiful, baby, but I think we'll save it for a *really* special occasion. We might have to get something else for the recital. Why don't you go up and change so nothing happens to it."

"Okay." She dutifully disappeared up the stairs, glitter rising in a puff behind her, just as Lee fell over backwards on the couch laughing uncontrollably.

"She cannot wear that."

"I told you."

"No, seriously, she looks like she's been overtaken by bats."

"What am I going to do?" Will was starting to panic.

"We've got to get her a new dress."

"We don't have *time*. There's no place to buy a dress in Berkeley—unless you want one handmade in the Himalayas from organic sheep's wool blessed by monks…I'd have a better chance of finding a recital sari."

"We'll have to go to the suburbs. Come on, let's roll."

They stood at the border of the children's clothing section of Macy's paralyzed by the choices in front of them. Brightly colored clothing hung in tight circular racks from one wall to the next in nauseating confusion. There were sale racks, designer racks, spring and summer and fall racks, racks of first-communion dresses and racks of dresses that looked like they were meant for 20-year olds.

"Jesus, this is why I shop on the web." From out of nowhere a sales clerk appeared to rescue them.

"Can I help you find something?"

"Yes." Will said with relief. "She needs a black dress."

"Sure thing," she said cheerily. She motioned to Jules, "Why don't you come with me and I'll help you try on some dresses. Your dads can wait here and you can show them when you're ready."

"That would be a huge help, thanks," Will said, ignoring the 'dads' comment. In a few minutes Jules appeared twirling out of the dressing room in an off-the-shoulder black velvet mini sheath dotted with rhinestones.

"No, I don't think that's the look we're going for." Will said, shocked at the sight of her little shoulders jutting out above the revealing neckline. Let's try another one." She tried on three more, spinning in front of them for their approval. All were creepily miniaturized versions of women's cocktail dresses.

"Are these designers all on CRACK?" Lee became loudly indignant.

"They're the latest styles." The salesgirl was defensive.

"For who? A cocktail lounge full of PEDOPHILES?"

"I don't think these are working," Will said quietly to the sales clerk.

"*No*, they are *NOT* working," Lee's voice was escalating, "What are we teaching these girls dressing them like they're TWENTY-EIGHT when they're *EIGHT*." Nearby shoppers began staring at them. The sales clerk looked like a fawn caught in the headlights. "I WANT TO TALK TO THE MANAGER OF THIS DEPARTMENT" Lee fumed.

"No, you don't." Will turned to the clerk. "We don't need to talk to the manager."

"I'M SERIOUS, WILL. THIS IS A COMMENTARY ON OUR WHOLE SOCIAL ETHOS."

"The recital is in one hour." Will tried to defuse his friend. "Why don't we take one of those dresses over there." He pointed to the chaste communion dresses with their puffed sleeves and lace petticoats.

The clerk looked annoyed. "Well, they're *white*...you said you wanted black..."

"It's okay, white is fine." He flipped through the rack quickly and grabbed the most innocent style he could find, ankle length with layers of white eyelet. "This looks perfect. Do you like this one, baby?"

Juliana's face lit up. "Yeah, it's pretty!"

"Great, let's have this one in her size and we're good to go." He threw down his credit card as fast as he could, and the sales woman rang them up sulkily, with Lee loudly continuing his social commentary to the customers nearby. Will hustled them out of the store through the nearest exit, Lee still fuming. After a few moments of silence in the car, Jules spoke up.

"Will?"

"What?"

"Do you think Miss Hopkins might be mad at me?" Will and Lee looked at each other, the realization sinking in that in a sea of young musicians clad in black clothing on the stage, Jules would be the only one dressed in pure communion white.

It was the therapist who first suggested Juliana take up a musical instrument. She wasn't recovering as well as her brother from the trauma of their parents' death. Danny had joined little league and soccer, thriving in the team play. It seemed to Will that he was never without a ball—kicking it down the hallway from his bedroom and out the door to the back yard, bouncing it against Maria's cottage wall, skirmishing endlessly in the yard with his friends until he was called in for supper—the ball seemed to offer an antidote for all the quiet worry he carried around.

Jules, on the other hand, had terrible separation anxiety whenever she was away from Will or her twin. She still wasn't eating well—each day Maria would scheme to pack a tantalizing lunch for her—sandwiches cut into animal shapes, sugary Mexican cookies frosted in colorful pastels—only to throw her arms up in frustration at the end of the day to find it all jumbled at the bottom of the lunchbox, uneaten. She lost interest in playing with other children, choosing instead to play games in her room in which she imagined their mother was still with them. She carried a small, jeweled picture frame with her mother's photo everywhere, setting a place for her at the table or in her playhouse. Once, when Will bought her new Barbie bedding, he came to her room late at night to see that she had lovingly laid out the pillow and comforter on one side of the bed, the corner turned down, the jeweled portrait smiling up from the pillow.

He tried to sign her up for team sports, but she was awful at them, which made going to games miserable for everyone involved. Almost every outing ended up in humiliation and tears, until he quietly stopped enrolling her. He tried gymnastics, but that was even worse. Will shuddered every time she stepped on a balance beam, her tiny frame teetering perilously on the four-inch plank of wood, until one day, unable to stand another excruciating second watching her poised to fall to the floor, he whisked her off the beam and out the door of the gym, never coming back.

But the violin was different. As soon as the teacher handed it to her, she seemed to light up. She cradled it gracefully. She liked bringing it to life, fingering the strings and running the bow across them to tease out sounds. Will never had to beg her to practice like other parents did, instead he would hear her up in her room playing the stanzas over and over until they sounded clear and lovely. She would close her eyes and listen to the notes, hardly ever glancing at the sheet music, playing solely from memory. It was more than memory, Will thought. She seemed to be drawing from a deep well of emotion, maybe even instinct, as though she was responding to an invisible genetic code handed down from her mother, as though Maria Gambiari was playing through her daughter.

They walked through the auditorium and dropped Jules off at her seat on the stage in all her first communion splendor, ignoring the gauntlet of disapproving looks from other parents. Lee, Will and Dan took their seats on folding chairs, dutifully applauding the squawking sounds of the student musicians as they paraded across the stage one after another to play their recital pieces with varying degrees of proficiency. Dan was placed between Lee and Will so they could muzzle his commentary as necessary.

On stage, Juliana sat calmly in her chair waiting her turn. She never displayed the usual anxiety of performing, it seemed to make her happy. When it was time, she walked to her spot and waved at her family, smiling easily, the white dress illuminating her under the stage lights. The pianist signaled to her to begin, and she put the violin to her shoulder and began to play Mozart's violin Concerto Number 5. She played by memory, with no sheet music, the notes beginning sweet and pure, building as she moved the bow slowly and delicately across the strings, pulling a rich, deep sound out of them that rose up and seemed to hover in the air around her, as if she was casting a spell. The rattling of chairs and chattering voices waned and the audience grew quiet. She looked angelic, Will thought, her eyes closed as though she was hearing the music before she played it, her slender body responding to each stroke of the bow as the notes grew more and more beautiful, more sensitive and supple. Time seemed suspended while she serenaded them, the audience now completely silent, rapt under her spell. When the last sweet note hung tantalizingly in the air, she opened her eyes and let the bow drop to her side, still cradling the violin. There was a brief pause, as if the room was collectively absorbing what had just happened, and then they began to applaud wildly, Lee, Will and Dan whooping and whistling along with them. Jules came out of her reverie and grinned, looking once again like a scrawny eight-year old. She sat back down in her chair, but the applause continued to swell, until her teacher gestured to her to come back out to take another bow. She walked onto the stage grinning, bending her head shyly, and rushed back to take her seat.

Afterward, when they went to Chez Panisse to celebrate, Jules was animated—talkative and radiant. As Will watched her giggling and gobbling down pizza he felt enormous relief. She'd found her true north.

Later that night, lying in bed in the dark, the inevitable panic set in.

"What?" Lee answered, half expecting the call. He knew the late night stillness always sent his friend's mind into overdrive.

"I had an epiphany."

"About what?"

"Jules. Watching her play tonight, I think… she might be better than I thought…"

"What was your first clue, her eidetic memory for music, or that she plays like an eight-year old Itzhak Perlman."

"Why didn't you say something?"

"Because I knew you would think this is one more thing you have to worry about."

"I *do*. I do have to worry about it. It's a *huge* responsibility."

"No it's not, Will. What's important is that it makes her happy. That's all that matters. As long as she's happy nothing you do or don't do can screw it up. Do you understand?"

"Yeah."

"She's going to be all right now."

Will was silent for a minute. "She plays like my mother."

"I know. I hear it too…get some sleep, buddy."

"Okay. Good night."

"Night."

eleven

"You're a big-shot surgeon now, are you sure you want to come home to live in the attic?"

"Yes, I'm *sure*. I want to help you with the kids, you've been doing it on your own all these years, it's time I step up."

"It's not all fun and games like it is when you're here on vacation, you know. It's a lot of hard work doing the day-to-day stuff—refereeing, helping with homework, disciplining..."

"I know, I want to do it."

"Okay, well God knows I can use the help," Will lied.

Dave was coming home from Boston for good. Dan and Jules were counting down the days until he arrived, dreaming up ambitious plans—ball games, camping, ferry rides—everything they missed doing with him when he lived away. Maria was frantically cleaning and preparing the upstairs studio and planning a menu of his favorite meals.

Will, on the other hand, was riddled with anxiety. His little household had fallen into its own circadian rhythms, and he worried about how his brother's presence would alter it. Dave was the "fun" brother—when he visited from Boston he came and went in a flash, bringing lavish gifts and initiating a frenzied week of activities with little discipline. No bedtime deadlines, no chores, no nutritional restrictions, just non-stop indulgence. The kids adored him, but by the time he left, Will and Maria had to spend the next week bringing them back down to earth.

To complicate matters, he was an accomplished orthopedic surgeon now. He'd accepted a job at a lucrative practice in Marin and he ran in heady social circles—including the women he dated. His declaration that he wanted to live in the old studio upstairs and help out with the kids was well-meaning, but Will doubted the quotidian nature of life on Avalon Street would hold allure for very long.

Lee offered to pick Dave up from his flight, mindful of Will's aversion to airports.

"So how is he doing, really? Dave queried, as they loaded the luggage into the car. "He never tells me much."

"He's okay. It's tough doing his job and raising two little kids, but he's got it handled."

"Does he have any personal life?"

"No. You know your brother. Everything he does is commando. It's pretty much work and kids, that's it."

"I hope that'll change now that I'm here to help out."

"I hope so too." Lee said, although he seriously doubted Dave was the guy to accomplish that.

The kids had been bouncing around the house all morning. They tracked Dave's plane from Boston on the laptop, hitting the refresh button manically to check his progress. They talked with him on his cell phone as the plane landed, again as got his luggage, and once more in Lee's car as he made his way home. By the time he walked through the door they were frantic, squealing and throwing their arms around him as he swung them around dizzily, their limbs locked together in the raucous affection of siblings.

Will stood back and watched them. They were all that was left of the world that was shattered when his parents died. When they were all together in the old house he felt the comfort he felt as a boy, when he innocently believed they would all be together forever. He threw his arms around Dave and hugged him hard. "It's good have you back," he grinned.

"It's good to be back." Dave surveyed his older brother at arms' length. He looked worn. "I brought you all something, Lee's getting it from the car." The kids were still hanging off of Dave as Lee walked through the door with a large refrigerated crate.

"What the…?"

"Lobsters! Live from Bah-ston. I'm going to cook them up for you, we can have a feast."

"No kidding?" Will was touched by the gesture. Maybe this *was* going to work out. He turned to Dan and Jules. "Go get Maria, she's been waiting all day for Dave to get here." They scurried out the door to the back cottage to get her.

"You look good," Dave said in the momentary calm of their absence. "A little tired."

"Yeah, the job, you know…"

"Pretty buff, have you been going to the gym?"

Will laughed out loud at the idea of fitting the gym into his insane schedule. "No, it's from keeping two 8-year olds out of harm's way."

"They look good, Will…"

"Doctor Dave!" Maria came bustling through the back door throwing her arms around him, kissing both cheeks. She held him away from her and looked him up and down approvingly. "Oh, you look so handsome!"

"And you look young and beautiful as ever." He hugged her tightly.

"Ohhhh, gracias," she said, brushing out imaginary wrinkles in her skirt as she soaked in the compliment. Will saw that she had changed into a newly sewn dress the color of mangos for Dave's arrival.

"I have lunch for you, mijo, you must be hungry. I'll go put it on the table!" She beamed and hurried into the kitchen. The kids were patiently waiting for their loot, trying their best to be polite.

"Have I forgotten anything? I don't think so…"

"Our presents!" Dan burst out.

"Oh, *that's* what I forgot." Dave teased. Bring my suitcase over here. They were all over him, helping him unzip his bags.

"This is for you," he handed Jules the iconic pink oblong box she so adored.

"Barbie! She squealed. "Look, Will, a Barbie!"

"Yeah, I see," Will grinned. She covered Dave in kisses and opened the box tenderly.

"That's not just any Barbie, that's a Betsy Ross Barbie. I don't think Betsy ever looked so shapely. And she has a flag and a sewing machine." Jules twirled around, holding the doll to her chest lovingly, and kissed her brother again.

"Thank you, she's beautiful!"

"You're welcome." Dave dug down and pulled out another larger package and handed it to Dan. And this is for you."

"Tyrannosaurus Rex!"

"Yeah, and see under here—push this button." Danny pushed a red button in its belly and it roared to life, turning its head and baring its teeth. The boy's eyes lit up and he threw his arms around Dave. "I'm glad you like them," Dave said softly, pulling both children into his chest and kissing them. Will could see his eyes welling. "It's good to be home."

For the rest of the afternoon and evening time stood still. They sat together around the old redwood table for hours talking and eating, Will and Dave telling stories about the old days to their attentive younger siblings, the kitchen filled with the aroma of Maria's enchiladas and warm, buttered flour tortillas. Will felt a sense of completeness he hadn't felt since his parents died. This was his family, home all together at last—however fleeting—in the house of his parents, and of his father's parents. He felt *happy*.

twelve

"What do you mean you wont be here until nine, that's too late, Dave." Will felt himself panicking for at least the third time that day. "It's *Christmas Eve*. We're supposed to be there by 5:00, everyone is expecting you." As he predicted, Dave's tenure at the house was short-lived. Weeknights spent at the Marin condo he bought "to avoid traffic" when he had early surgeries soon stretched into weekends. Before long he was an infrequent visitor to the Avalon house, begging off with work or a social engagement. Even worse, he was dating a woman Will despised—a wealthy, manipulative scion of an old San Francisco family. His life was dominated by toney cocktail parties, yacht club outings, and trumped up charity events designed to give the seriously rich an excuse to dress up and bask in their own glow. Now, once again, he was bailing on the family at the last minute.

"Stop panicking, you'll do fine without me, just explain to Eleanor that I got tied up with a patient."

"Really, a *patient*? Is her name Heather?"

"I just got tied up."

"We need to present a united front, Dave. You know how Eleanor is about these events." Will got a knot in his stomach imagining his grandmother opening the door and seeing that Dave was missing. "Besides, the kids are expecting you, they've been talking about you coming all day." Jules came running into the kitchen as if to punctuate Will's point.

"Is he almost here?" She was fidgeting excitedly in her socks and slip as Maria followed her, trying to brush her curls into a ponytail.

"He's coming a little later, baby." Will handed the phone to Jules and walked out of the room to collect himself. Let Dave explain to her why he couldn't show up to Christmas Eve dinner, he was tired of covering for him. He went upstairs to change into a shirt and tie. He thought about Christmas eve when he was a boy, the anticipation of going to his grandmother's house and seeing the enormous Christmas tree shooting up between the pair of spiral staircases, bursting with lights and ornaments, the brightly wrapped presents spilling tantalizingly out from under it.

"Too much, mom!" Henry Thompkins would always say when he saw the pile of gifts.

"Nonsense!" She would fire back, gleefully. "There's no point having grandchildren if you can't spoil them."

Now, for Will, Christmas eve at Oakhaven was a trial to be endured until they could return home to Avalon Street, to their tree strung with popcorn garlands and handmade yarn sheep and popsicle-stick sleighs and other undecipherable paper mache concoctions the kids had made in school that hung alongside the treasured ornaments from their parents' Christmases past. He couldn't wait for the ordeal to be over so they could wake up in their own beds, in the familiar old house they had all grown up in, with its beamed ceilings and creaking wood floors; to their own celebration spent lazing in their pajamas playing with new toys, eating their traditional Christmas morning breakfast of pancakes and strawberry jam, around the great redwood table felled by lightening that was Will's touchstone to his parents and to the generations before him.

"Any chance you're free tonight?" Will struggled to hide the anxiety in his voice.

"Dave bailed?"

"Yeah."

"Sure. Let me get my suit out of mothballs." Lee seldom wore anything besides Hawaiian shirts and t-shirts he had collected from various road trips, boasting locations like "Buzby's Texas Barbeque" and "Every T'ing Cool Jamaican Bar." He was a brilliant internist, but he had absolutely no pretensions and no particular interest in money. He once turned down a lucrative offer of a partnership at a high-end practice at Stanford because he found out they had a dress code.

"Can you imagine having to wear a shirt and tie every day?" He told Will incredulously. *"It's outrageous."*

"It's a 500K a year partnership, you sure you can't compromise?"

"Nah, that's an obscene amount of money for any doctor to make anyway. I like my patients. They're a little down at the heels, but at least they don't care what I wear."

Will lined up his children at the bottom of the stairs for inspection. Maria stood by tentatively in case any adjustments had to be made.

"Okay, let's make sure we got everything right. You're wearing grandma's gold necklace she gave you for your birthday. Good. And this is the dress and shoes she sent from Saks, right?"

"Si" Maria knew the drill.

"Perfect, you look beautiful, baby," he planted a kiss on her forehead. Jules smiled, relieved to pass inspection.

Will turned to Danny and patted down his unruly curls. "You look handsome in that new jacket and tie, babe, your grandmother is going to be so proud of you."

"This tie kind of chokes me, Will."

"I know, son, it's what ties do. You might as well get used to it. As soon as we get there you can take it off, okay?"

"Okay."

"All right, we're ready for battle. Kiss Maria goodbye, she's got to get to Margarita's so she can start her own Christmas." They had celebrated earlier that morning with Maria, and now she gathered up the gifts they'd given her to take to the farm in Gilroy for a much-needed rest. Will hugged her and watched her make her way out the door to the car, the children trailing behind carrying her presents and suitcase. She wore a hand-made dress of bright red and green holly leaves dotted with prancing reindeer; a matching, miniature version hung lovingly in the closet waiting for Jules to wear Christmas day.

"Drive carefully!" Will called out, his stomach tightening as she got farther from the house. Just as they were waving off Maria's station wagon, Lee appeared walking across the lawn from his house. The sight of his friend dressed nattily in his suit snapped him out of his mood.

"You clean up nicely." Will smiled.

"Let's not kid ourselves, it's like putting a tuxedo on a pig." Lee grinned back.

When they arrived in Atherton the guard let them through the great iron gate and they left the car in the circular driveway with the valet.

"Welcome back, Dr. Thompkins, Merry Christmas."

"Thanks Jess, Merry Christmas to you too." Jess had worked for his grandmother since Will was a boy. One thing about Eleanor, she was loyal.

"Have fun," Jess smiled wryly.

"We'll try." Will smiled. He lined up his children for inspection a last time, patting down Danny's hair again and adjusting his tie. "Remember, we're not going to talk about the whole roof-climbing incident, right?"

"Right."

"Or Jules going down the laundry chute."

"Uh huh."

"And nothing about the dog biting the meter reader."

"It wasn't Otis's fault, he scared him."

"I know, but we're not going to talk about it, okay?"

"Okay."

"High five, we're goin' in." The four of them slapped hands and headed for the front door. "May the force be with us."

"There are my loves!" Eleanor answered the door herself, no doubt informed by gate security that they had arrived. She threw her arms tightly around her grandchildren and kissed them repeatedly. "Look at you, you've grown since I saw you last month! Juliana you are as beautiful as your mother, and Daniel, you look so handsome, just like your father." They both beamed, basking in the affection of their grandmother. Will chastised himself for his churlishness. This was why he brought them here. To connect to this place and to their grandmother the way he had as a child.

"Will, you're late."

"I know, we had last minute things come up, sorry."

"Where is Dave?" Will's stomach tightened.

"He got hung up in Marin, he wont be able to make it."

"Shame on him. I'll give him a piece of my mind later."

Please do, Will thought darkly.

"I see you brought a suitable substitute, Hello Lee." She hugged him warmly. How is the practice going?"

"Not bad. In spite of my mismanagement."

"My offer stands to get my accountant to look at your books. You don't have to starve to be a good doctor you know."

"I just might take you up on that." He laughed.

She leaned down to kiss the children again, "All right, go in and have fun, there are lots of surprises for you inside." Their faces lit up as they eyed the enormous tree. Dancers from the San Francisco Ballet—Clara and the Sugar Plum fairy and the Nutcracker and an assortment of dancing bears and tin soldiers—were swirling around the room entertaining the guests.

"You have outdone yourself this year," Will said, hugging her and taking in all the festivities.

"There's no point having grandchildren if you're not going to spoil them!" She said, clearly delighted with herself.

Two scotches later, the knot in his stomach was gone and he was finally at ease, slumped in a chair enjoying the relief of having gotten through another trial. The party really was something to behold. No detail had been spared. The tree was spectacularly aglow with ornaments and lights. Dancers twirled through the guests in their glittery, confectionary costumes, strolling musicians serenaded the crowd, and butlers in white tuxedoes served trays of champagne and food. It was a child's dream of what Christmas should be. When all was said and done, he was grateful for his grandmother's effusive affection, however difficult their relationship was at times. He was grateful his children had the opportunity to bask in the warmth of it. He saw them both across the room, kneeling under the boughs of the Christmas tree shaking packages excitedly, eyes lit with anticipation. He glanced over to see Lee entertaining Eleanor with some humorous story, probably bawdy, her shoulders shaking with laughter. He rested his head back on his chair and gazed up at the frescoes of seraphim above him. There were times he thought they were cruelly ironic, frozen in their eternal state of heavenly bliss while the world underneath them had writhed in pain like some frieze from a renaissance depiction of hell. But tonight he found solace in their unwavering state of joy. Time was healing him. Maybe Lee was right. Maybe he *was* lucky.

thirteen

"That's Simon, get the door!" Jules called down in a panic from upstairs. Will was on his laptop in the living room in his favorite leather chair, once his father's chair, that his two teenagers now referred to as "his post," a reference to the fact he could survey the staircase and the front door in one sweep, monitoring their coming and going.

It was prom night, a thinly veiled yearly attempt to get parents to fork out enormous amounts of money while teenagers flirted, courted, schemed, shopped, gossiped, cried, back-stabbed, and shopped some more in an attempt to fulfill a ritualistic rite of passage that in Will's mind should have been jettisoned in the 50s. Limousines, corsages, fancy dinners, expensive dresses, rented ballrooms, surreptitious attempts to sneak in alcohol, it was all so bloated now that Will wondered how it didn't collapse under its own weight. Mix in a healthy dose of Berkeley's self-conscious multiculturalism and the result was a teenage mardi gras on steroids.

Will got to the door just as Jules did. He had already grilled Dan days before on her date, who he had not yet met.

"He nice, he's...kind of edgy." Dan had squirmed a little, like a bug held down by pins on an exhibit board.

"Edgy? What does that mean? Edgy like taking drugs edgy? Been to prison edgy?"

"No, of course not. He's nice. Really. He's in my AP Biology class. He's just got kind of an edgy style."

Will opened the door to see a tall skinny goth kid dressed head to toe in black. His jet black hair was spiked into little daggers. He had black eyeliner under his eyes and piercings on his nose, lip and eyebrow. A neck tattoo of a bleeding skull was sneaking out above the collar of his black pleated tuxedo shirt. Will slammed the door shut.

"What are you doing? It's Simon!" Jules shouted, alarmed.

"NO." He called out, to no one in particular.

"Will, open this door immediately!" Jules was panicked. Now they both had their hands gripped on the doorknob, Will battling for the soul of his little girl with Beelzebub at the gate.

"Will!" Juliana got a grip on his hand and turned the knob to pull the door open. She had the advantage of not being in 'stunned' mode.

"Hello Dr. Thompkins, It's nice to meet you," the boy put out his tattooed hand to shake Will's. "I'm Simon Rosen. Remember me?"

Will numbly shook his hand and looked straight into the eyes of pure evil. "No, I can't say I do."

"My dad is Ethan Rosen, he's a surgeon at Mercy...I went to grade school with Jules. I've changed my look a little." He smiled, the ring on his lip stretching as he did.

"You're Ethan's boy?" Will vaguely remembered him now, a geeky little fourth grader with a yarmulke. He peered out behind Simon's dark visage to the car parked in front of the house. It looked innocent enough, a silver Minicooper.

"I have my license, my provisional period is over, so I'm legal to drive Jules by myself."

"I see."

"Jules, you look beautiful!" He called out to her across the doorway, Will's body still blocking the threshold. Jules pinched Will and pressed her body against him to move him out of the way. *She was only 90 pounds! Did Simon give her superhuman strength with his vampire bite?*

"Thanks, so do you! That's a great tux." He pushed past Will and presented her with a small wrist corsage of pastel flowers. "Oh, they're beautiful," she said with a sweet smile. *Did she look paler than usual?*

"I've got yours in the fridge, let me get it, come on in and sit down." She turned to Will and whispered loudly in his ear, "*Talk* to him!"

Will attempted to make small talk, instead fixating on the skull tattoo, which seemed to squint menacingly at him above his collar whenever the boy moved his head.

"This is a very nice house." Simon said, his eyebrow earring lifting up and down as he spoke. I've always liked this neighborhood. It has a great history. *Was he eyeing the house with some unholy plan?*

"Here it is." Jules returned with lightening speed, attaching the corsage to his tuxedo lapel. Just then Lee walked through the front door, camera in hand.

"Sorry I'm late, I forgot to charge my battery," he said, stopping dead in his tracks at the image of Simon sitting on the couch next to Jules. "Who are YOU?" He demanded unceremoniously.

"This is Simon Rosen, my date. Simon, this is Lee Calahan, my dad's best friend. He works at Mercy too."

"Pleased to meet you Mr. Calahan." Simon once again put out a tattooed hand, but Lee was too stunned to reciprocate.

"Simon's dad is Ethan Rosen," Will offered, trying to justify to his best friend why he was letting his little girl be taken to the prom by the Prince of Darkness.

Lee just stared back at him, for once completely mute himself.

"We have to get going soon, do you want to take the pics now?" Jules offered, trying to hasten their escape.

"Does his image actually show up on film?" Lee muttered under his breath to Will as the teenagers positioned themselves against the fireplace for a photo op.

After the photos, for most of which Lee aimed the camera on Jules, they sent her off into the silver Minicooper, Will with his hands gripped on the door handle and window frame in a futile effort to keep the car from moving forward, sternly laying down instructions about curfew as they pulled away, Juliana waving back at them, silently mouthing "I love you" through the window as she hastily rolled it up.

"Is he *safe*?" Lee was uncharacteristically alarmist as they walked back into the house.

"I don't know. He seemed polite enough. Ethan's a good guy. I don't think there's enough time at a prom to lure her into a satanic cult."

"*Are* there Jewish Satanic cults?"

"I have no idea." Will slumped into his chair. "This whole teenage thing has got me completely thrown off my parenting game. I don't know whether I'm supposed to be cool and let them experiment or lock them in their rooms."

"How does a guy like Ethan have a kid like that?"

"Ethan is a fallen soldier in the parenting army, *that's* how. It could happen to any one of us."

"Where's Dan? Isn't he supposed to come here before he leaves with his date?"

"They went to her house first. It's a new girl, Elizabeth. She's driving. She's *sixteen*," he said, as though she was an ex-convict. "I've never met her. I met Kelly, but she was *last* week. His girl-friends have the shelf life of a ripe tomato."

On cue Dan came through the front door with his date, a leggy brunette in a gold lame micro-mini. They went through the usual pleasantries, Lee taking pictures, Will interrogating the girl with thinly veiled small talk in which he attempted to extract information about her background and their plans for the night. Before they left he pulled Dan into the kitchen for a final grilling.

"Do you have your wallet?"

"Yes."

"Cell phone?"

"Yup."

"It stays ON *at all times.*"

"Check."

"No bullshit excuses about the battery being dead, or not seeing my texts. I know you're tied to that phone like crack cocaine."

"Got it."

Okay, "I just want to go over the plan." He locked his gaze on him. "You are out of the dance at midnight. It takes about 15 minutes to get from the Claremont hotel to Zachary's Pizza. I'll give you 30 if there's traffic getting out of the parking lot. That gives you 1.0 hours to have pizza and get home by 1:30. That is the drop-dead curfew. Are we clear on that?"

"Yes."

"It takes 10 minutes to get home from Zachary's. No excuses. I know the route."

"Maybe you'd like to ride in the back seat, Dr. Will." Dan teased.

"Don't be a wise ass, I would if I could. I'd plant a GPS chip in you if it was legal. Now give me a hug and I wont embarrass you in front of Elizabeth." He put his arms around him and held him in a long hug.

"I gave up being embarrassed by this family's public displays of affection a long time ago."

"Good, because they're not going to stop." Will kissed him on both cheeks and cupped his hand on his head. "Now go and have fun. But not *too much* fun."

"Will do."

"And keep an eye on your sister and the goth prince, will you?"

"Will do."

"I need a drink." Will said grabbing two beers from the fridge.

"Did you see that girl's dress?" Lee asked, incredulous.

"What there was of it, yes." Will took a long gulp of beer. "Whatever happened to those beautiful ball gowns girls used to wear to proms? When did the prom become a booty call?"

"I don't know, but I am definitely getting old. I had the urge to cover her up with a blanket." They downed the beers and went for a second round. Will's mind went into its usual overdrive.

"I think I gave them too much time before curfew. If the dance goes to midnight they have a full hour to have sex, get to Zachary's, eat a fast piece of pizza and come home like nothing happened. That dress is an 'I want to have sex with you' dress. It's like an engraved invitation to a 14-year-old boy who's a bag of hormones."

"Let it go, Will, there's nothing you can do about it."

"Do you think he has a condom? She's *sixteen*, she looks like she's been around the block a few times. Maybe I should have slipped one in his tux."

"Come on, let's shoot some hoops." They went out into the chilly night to play, the rhythmic slapping of the ball on the pavement working its usual magic on Will.

"Where is Dave? I thought he wanted to be here." Lee queried, popping the ball into the basket from across the driveway.

"He's with his lawyer. Heather pulled some new stunt, they're going over the paperwork."

"Jesus, is this divorce ever going to end?"

"Not if she can help it."

"Damn he was blind."

"He's a big boy, he was warned. I just hope she doesn't bleed him dry."

"I've got to tell you, it definitely put me off marriage after seeing what happened to him."

Will stopped dribbling the ball and stared at him. "Like you were considering it? You don't date a woman longer than 3 months."

"I consider it. Some time in the future."

"Really? Wow, I had no idea. Kids?"

"I love kids. Well…I love *your* kids." Lee grinned.

Will stopped short and looked at his friend intently. "You'd make a great father. You should think about it."

"What about you?" Lee fired back.

"Nah, it's not in the cards for me."

"Why?"

"You said it a long time ago. I'm lucky. I got these kids. I'm not going back to the well again, that's just tempting fate."

"So that's it? You're not looking to find someone?"

Will continued dribbling the ball, slapping it hard against the pavement. "This family was granted one great love affair, and I got the legacy from that. I'm not asking for anything else,"

"So if the right person came along you wouldn't take a leap of faith?"

Will stopped in his tracks and stared coldly into his friend's eyes. "I took a leap of faith. I put my parents on a plane to Italy."

Lee took the ball from him and threw it for a shot. He knew when Will was done with a conversation. He didn't want to open that wound again, even after all these years it bled too close to the surface. They played silently for more than an hour, until the cold and damp finally drove them indoors. Lee headed home, pensive about their conversation. Will settled at his post to wait for his children to come back home safely.

The next morning, as Will leaned against the counter drinking coffee and reading the newspaper, Dave walked tentatively into the kitchen. Will knew something was wrong immediately by the look on his face. He loved his brother, but after years of watching him make poor decisions about his personal life, he found it hard to be sympathetic to his predicaments.

"How'd it go with the lawyer last night?"

"Not good." Dave looked shaken.

"How not good?"

"She's… come up with a new demand. It's bullshit, but my attorney thinks she might have some traction with it."

Will's antenna went up. "What is it?"

"It's complicated."

"Try me."

Dave looked away from his brother's piercing gaze. "It involves my share of this house."

Will felt a wave of nausea pass through him. "What do you mean your share of this house? Why would she have *anything* to do with this house?"

"It's a long story. I signed some documents when we got married…it's complicated."

Will was stunned into silence. The house was nearly as sacrosanct to him as his children. He was its caretaker, the keeper of its legacy, the surrogate for his great-great grandfather who bought it, for his parents who cherished it. He imagined Heather heaving an axe into the redwood table to take away her share. The anger welled up in him. "This house has been in the family for four generations—you were married to that woman for five years."

"I'm aware of that, Will."

"What kind of 'documents' could you have possibly signed that would let her into this house?"

"You're not making it any easier."

"I'm not trying to make it easier. Your whole fucking life has been easy. What kind of documents did you sign?" Will felt himself becoming unhinged with rage.

"It was a pre-nup." Dave stepped back, waiting for his brother's censure. "I understand you're angry, I don't blame you."

"No, you *don't* understand. This isn't about me being angry. You need to *fix* this. Get another lawyer, get a dozen fucking lawyers, and *fix* it. No one is threatening this house."

Dave saw a look in his brother's eyes he'd never seen. "I'm working on it, we have an estate attorney looking into it."

Will felt his chest tighten at the word "estate." *Eleanor.* Any legal inquiry into the estate would alert Eleanor's lawyers. He felt sick to his stomach. All the years of keeping his grandmother at bay. He felt like his whole world was crushing in on him. He suddenly had an uncontrollable urge to punch his brother. He wanted to hit him for all the flimsy excuses, for all the times Dan and Jules waited excitedly for him to show up only to be let down when the inevitable phone call came, for all the late nights sitting up with a sick kid while Dave slept blissfully unaware, for all the times he had to joust with Eleanor alone because Dave was off sailing, or fucking some woman he met at a cocktail party. Will grabbed his brother by one shoulder and let his fist fly into his jaw. Dave was stunned, caught off guard by his brother's ferocity. He reeled back into the kitchen counter and Will let another punch fly. Now he wanted to hurt him—for threatening his house, his children, his parents' legacy. Dave recovered and fought back, but he was no match for Will, who was wild with fury now, pummeling his brother as they wrestled across the kitchen,

The back door opened and Lee walked in for his customary Sunday breakfast, stunned to find Dave pinned against the redwood table with Will throwing punches at him.

"What the—?" He wrapped his arms around Will and pulled him off his brother. Will resisted, digging in his heels, his fists flying in the air as Dave slid away from the table out of his reach. Lee pushed Will's shoulders hard against the wall and held him there with both arms, yelling at Dave to get out of the room. Will was wild-eyed, still hungry for blood, staring through his friend to Dave as he stumbled out of the kitchen. Lee held him tight, trying to talk him down, "The kids are going to wake up. You don't want them to see the two of you beating each other up." Will shook his head and stared at him with slow recognition. Lee continued to hold him against the wall, wary of his next move, until at last Will slumped under his grip. As he felt the adrenalin leave his body, Lee slowly released him. "What the fuck happened?"

Will rubbed his jaw where a punch landed. "I can't...I can't talk about it."

"I find you two beating the shit out of each other in the kitchen—you're going to talk about it."

"The divorce...Heather wants a share of this house."

"What...how? She can't possibly have any right to this house, it's an inheritance, he owned it before he married her."

"Apparently she does. He's signed some kind of a pre-nup, I don't know the details, I was too pissed to get the whole story."

"Jesus Christ." Lee went silent, trying to take in the ramifications.

"His lawyer is bringing in an estate attorney. It's only a matter of time before Eleanor finds out."

"Shit."

"Yeah. That's going to be a nice conversation." Will rubbed his hand over his head trying to pull himself together. He caught a glimpse of Dave standing in the doorway of the kitchen, blood dripping from his nose and lip, his eye beginning to swell where Will's fist connected. His anger started to turn to regret. Dave walked into the room and faced his brother head on.

"I *am* going to fix it, Will. No matter what it takes."

"Family first, Dave. That's the rule. This family always comes first. You put us at risk,"

"I know, I fucked up, but I'm not the selfish asshole you think I am. I may not always rise to your standards, but I love this family too." There was a long uneasiness as they stood staring at each other. Lee broke the silence.

"You guys might want to clean up before Dan or Jules get up, or you're going to have some explaining to do."

Dave wiped the blood from his face. "I've got to go, I don't want them to see me like this."

"What's next?" Will could barely contain his contempt.

"We're meeting with the estate attorney this afternoon."

"Eleanor is going to find out."

"I know. I'll deal with her." Dave looked away from both of them. "I better go." He paused for a moment at the door. "Did they…have a good time at the prom?"

"Yeah, they had fun."

Dave turned to Lee, his right eye now nearly closed from the swelling. "Thanks for saving my other eye."

"No problem." Lee said.

They watched him slip out through the back door of the kitchen into the chilly morning air.

fourteen

Will walked into the Slanted Door restaurant not knowing what the night had in store for him. It had been six years since he and Miranda Holloway had seen each other. His late night phone call to her had rekindled mixed feelings of insecurity and attraction. He reserved a booth facing the lights of the bay and ordered a bottle of Chateau Margaux, her favorite, to be waiting at the table when she arrived.

He thought about all the things in his life that had changed since he'd last been in the Slanted Door. It was Katrina's favorite restaurant. They would meet here in those painful early days after his parents' death. They would order wine and small plates, filling the table with fragrant delicacies, eating and drinking as they told each other their latest stories. Afterward, she would take him home to her bed where she would wrap him in the silky folds of her body, healing the gaping wounds that exposed him to the world. He was so broken then, so raw. He wished he knew where she was so he could thank her for getting him through those times. He would tell her he was better now, that his work made him happy and his children were growing strong and healthy. He gazed out the window to the silvery bay with its ships headed off to distant ports and wondered what had become of her—was she married now, did she have her own children? Or was she still traversing the world, a free spirit with no ties to anyone. His reverie was broken by the sudden appearance of Miranda standing in front of him. She was dressed in a shimmering gold halter top and a short black skirt, her blonde hair swept up in a soft knot at the nape of her neck complementing her bronzed shoulders. She was more beautiful than he remembered, a little older now, her face more sculpted and expressive.

"Wow. Look at you." He said, embracing her and kissing her cheek." Beautiful as ever."

"You look pretty beautiful yourself," She said affectionately, kissing him back. She put her hand up to his face and the soft jingle of her gold bracelets filled his ear seductively.

They made small talk, catching up on each other's lives. She was even more successful now, but less self-conscious about proving it. She had come into her own, and there was a quiet confidence about her that made her more appealing, less intimidating.

Will was at ease as they spent the evening talking over his brother's case, filling her in on the details that weren't visible in the paperwork he had sent her—the personalities, the motives, the vulnerability of his father's hastily-created trust. He confided to her his overriding fear of the house being compromised in any way and she was compassionate, nothing like the old Miranda who might have balked at such sentimentality. But she was also diamond sharp—incisive and tactical, asking questions, absorbing details, coalescing every nuance and fact into an integrated plan of attack. No wonder she was so successful, he thought, she was brilliant at law. They talked for hours, lingering over the wine and food, watching the soft glow of the fog hugging the Bay Bridge, its string of lights glimmering across the water. They stretched out the evening as long as they could, dessert, aperitifs, espresso, until there was no more reason to linger. As he paid the bill and the last dishes were cleared, Will found himself once again under her spell. He wanted her, but he couldn't bring himself to suggest it. As always, Miranda took charge.

"Would you like to come up to my place?" She smiled.

"I would love that." He said, her words arousing him.

She had taken a car service to the restaurant, so he drove her in his Porsche, grateful he hadn't brought the old Volvo station wagon he used to cart the kids around, its seats filled with lacrosse sticks, old sweatshirts and sticky candy wrappers. They drove up to the glass monolith, the valet greeting them and taking the car. Miranda put her hand in his as they made their way through the lobby, an uncharacteristically affectionate gesture for her, and he responded by wrapping his arm around her waist and pulling her toward him, the smell of perfume in her hair arousing his senses as much as the sight of her bare shoulder as she nestled under him. By the time they got to her private elevator they made no pretense to hide the attraction. As they watched the doorman's face disappear behind the closing elevator doors, they came crushing together with lips and arms passionately fondling each other, his erection now in full force, pressing against her as she pulled him toward her, reaching to undo his belt as the elevator whisked up through the 60 floors to her apartment. By the time the door opened to her foyer they were half naked, her skirt up around her waist, her breasts cupped in his hands, the nipples hard in his hungry mouth.

He was mad for her, stumbling to get his pants off to get inside her. Her black lace underwear was slid down to reveal her taught, bare abdomen. They managed to shed the rest of their clothing and make their way to the downy white rug, where he laid her down gently, his mouth all over her, craving her body. She raised herself up to him, relishing the feel of his mouth on her, stroking him as he hungrily played with her between his teeth. They teased each other as long as they could bear it, until he was begging her to let him have her. When she finally did, his body was on fire as he pressed into her, feeling her take him in. He rolled over as she raised her hips to take him deeper, until at last he released into her in a torrent of lust. They laid there for a few minutes, briefly sated, but then feeling her hands gently stroking him, the lust returned. He leaned over and they began kissing passionately again, this time she pulled him to her bedroom where they continued their sexual exploits, taking advantage of the comfort of her enormous bed and the luxury of performing any acrobatics they wanted.

When it was over, they were beyond spent. They drifted in and out of sleep oblivious to their surroundings until morning, their bodies twisted together in post coital exhaustion. At last the sun came flooding over them, unfiltered by the blinds which they hadn't bothered to close. Will found his pants, dropped unceremoniously by the elevator door, and pulled them on, putting on his t-shirt that he found a few feet away. He made coffee, Miranda still asleep, and dragged one of the Mies van der Rohe chairs to the window so he could enjoy the view of the city. It was a clear morning, and he could see all the way across the bay to Berkeley, where he knew his children were probably still asleep. He was amazed at how different things looked from Miranda's vantage point. His world, the house on Avalon Street, the hospital, the familiar streets and shops and restaurants of Berkeley that constituted his universe were only a speck in the vast vista that was her everyday existence. He was ruminating about the smallness of his life when he felt her arms wrap around him from behind. She planted a kiss on his neck and came around to kneel in front of him, resting her arms on his knees and looking into his eyes. It was a tender gesture he couldn't imagine the old Miranda making. He leaned over to kiss her and she lifted her head to meet him.

"Mmmm. Coffee." She smiled, tasting it on his lips.

"I'll get you some, stay there," he offered. But she was already up padding into the kitchen to get her own. She pulled up the other Mies next to him and the two of them sat staring out at the view lazily making small talk. Neither of them had anywhere immediately to go, so they whipped up some eggs and toast and juice and watched the city and the bay come alive as the morning progressed. Finally, Miranda confessed she had a hair appointment she should keep, and Will knew it was time to get back home, so he kissed her goodbye, stepping into the elevator with her still in her robe, throwing him a kiss as the elevator door closed on her lovely face. There was no talk of what would come next. That was Miranda, always in charge.

Up in the glass palace he felt like an astronaut, weightless, far away from the reality of his daily life. But as the elevator lowered him back to earth, gravity resumed, and the weight of his troubles began to bear down on him again. Things were more strained than ever with his brother.

The estate lawyer was not successful. Dave's pre-nup seemed to be iron-clad. They had made an attempt to buy Heather out with an outrageous sum, but she wasn't interested in the money, she wanted her pound of flesh. She loved twisting the knife into the family slowly, causing just enough pain and suffering without killing her prey, and she had bottomless wealth to keep the game afoot. She would drag out every legal parry with absurd delays and frivolous new demands. Worse, she would show up at the house unannounced, rattling everyone's nerves. At first they tried to be polite, thinking they could win her with kindness and reason, but eventually they had to get a restraining order. Then she sent a private investigator, who would park across the street watching their comings and goings. Dave stopped visiting the house, hoping to draw away the fire, but it didn't help. Heather was a prominent socialite, and the gossip blogs swirled with her sensational accusations, regularly posting salacious "leaked" details of their personal life, prompting reporters to show up on the lawn snapping photos of them all. Dave's professional reputation was taking a beating.

Dave blamed himself for putting the family at risk and Will wasn't inclined to forgive him. Eleanor was livid when she learned what he had done, refusing to help. Instead, sensing a chink in the armor at last, she refortified her efforts to have Dan and Jules come and live with her in Atherton where they weren't exposed to such vagaries. She had gone so far as to initiate their enrollment in an expensive private school, Pembroke, in an effort to force Will's hand. In spite of everyone's best efforts, Dan and Jules were caught in the middle, feeling the pressure to make everyone they loved happy, with no clue how to navigate the chess game where they were the prize.

His only solace was work. He was the Chief of Emergency Medicine now, Rob had retired, and he relished the opportunity to run the ER with his own stamp. He promoted Carlotta, and together they were instituting changes they'd talked about for years that were proving to be wildly successful. Wait times were shortened, new equipment—wrangled out of donors and hospital administrators by way of Carlotta's persuasive charms—along with digital charting and better treatment protocols had improved patient care, and a new recruitment program for residents was bringing fresh, bright talent to the ER. He was a hands-on Chief, spending time in the trenches treating patients whenever he could. The residents and interns were afraid of him, but they were becoming good doctors, and he felt satisfaction that he was sending them out into the world like medical missionaries to do good work at other hospitals and other ERs.

His passion for emergency medicine was a driving force in his life. Some doctors craved the adrenalin rush of the ER, but for Will it was much more than that. It was the chance to rescue people when they were at their most vulnerable, when they were wounded and afraid and giving themselves up to him for help. He was passionate about emergency medicine because in each patient, in that decisive moment they were surrendered to him, he saw a fresh a chance to save his parents.

Dan and Jules nagged him constantly about dating, trying to set him up with the mothers of their friends, shopkeepers, nurses, teachers, but in truth it was a lot easier having a moribund love life. Jules said he was afraid of commitment, but how much more committed could he be? He was dedicated to his children, he was a loyal friend, he worried over his patients as if they were his own family. It was Dave who had the commitment problem. He bounced in and out of their lives with no thought to the messes he left behind.

And *yet*, after nights like last night, with Miranda, he realized how much more at ease he was with a woman. It wasn't just the sex, although god knows that was great. When he was with a woman he felt, however fleeting, that someone was taking care of *him*, that he wasn't alone trying to hold the plane up in the air to keep it from falling out of the sky.

He walked into the house to hear the sound of Juliana's violin playing the theme from *Cinema Paradiso*. It was a favorite piece his mother played that always brought his father to tears. Will loved it too, although it was so exquisitely beautiful when his mother played it that he couldn't understand why it made his father sad.

"Mono no aware," Henry Thompkins explained to his boy. "'Beautiful sadness.' It's a Japanese aesthetic principle —the most beautiful things in life also bring us sorrow, because we know they're fleeting."

When he was young, Will tried hard to hold these two ideas in his head, but his life was so full, stretched out in front of him in a vista of endless possibilities, that he never quite understood. As he got older, the meaning of those words resonated. He thought about his parents' brief vibrant life, evaporated in an instant in a crush of mangled metal and fire, about his moments of triumph in the ER followed inevitably by equally painful losses, about the joy of raising his children, watching them grow, knowing they were simultaneously slipping away from him like sand through his fingers. "Mono no aware."

Juliana's violin got softer as she heard him come in, until he heard her put it down and come looking for him.

"Did you have to work the night shift?" She asked, worried.

"Yeah, just checking on my interns. Everything go okay here?"

"Yeah. Maria and I made up a new recipe for dinner. I was hoping maybe you were out on a date..."

"No such luck," he lied. He never let his children know about his nights away, as infrequent as they were.

"That was a pretty piece you were playing."

"It's from *Cinema Paradiso.*"

"I know. You play it just the way mom used to play it." Jules' face lit up. She loved being reminded that she was Maria Gambiari's daughter.

"Grandma called."

Will's stomach tightened. *Gravity.*

"She's really serious about Pembroke, Will. She was talking about how good it was and how nice the kids are there, and that we could come to Berkeley on weekends, Harry would take us anywhere we want." Harry was Eleanor's driver. She was upping the ante now. He felt as though a Trojan horse was at his front door, and he wasn't sure who was going to come charging out of it—Heather or Eleanor.

"Don't worry. She's…just trying to do what she thinks is best for you."

"I don't want to leave here Will. It's my *Mole End*," she said plaintively, referring to the little abode of her favorite character in *Wind in the Willows*. When she was a child, Will would read the book to her again and again to comfort her at night. She never got tired of hearing about Mole and Rat's vagabond adventures, which always ended safely at hearth and home, with the glow of a warm fire and fuzzy slippers and a sumptuous dinner set at their table. He often wondered if she identified with them because they were orphans, little creatures set about in the big world to fend for themselves, banded together to make the best of their situation.

"What character would you be if you could be in the book," Will once asked her.

"I'd be Mole," she said without hesitation, "He loves his home and his little valley and his friends. Which character would you want to be?"

"Ratty," Will said, without hesitation. "Setting off in a boat down the river to new adventures."

"Really?" She looked surprised.

"Why, who do you think I should be?"

"I think of you as Badger," she said, "You know, very sensible, everyone relies on him, a little grumpy, but very wise, and kind."

Will laughed. "Of course he's grumpy, he's got to rescue everyone all the time." He teased. He's the only animal with good sense!"

"Mole has good sense!" She countered. He talks Ratty out of running off to sea." Will smiled at his little girl, always so afraid to leave him, afraid to leave home, crawling into Danny's bed at night to curl up next to him in a primal need for security. Even now, growing up, she was trying her best to go out into the big world, her music taking her to places she wouldn't have dreamed of going before, but she was always happiest at home among the walls of the old house full of her favorite things and the comforting memories of her parents.

"Miss Eleanor called!" It was Maria snapping him out of his reverie, bursting out of the kitchen in a bright turquoise dress, waving her spoon, trailing the aroma of Mexican spices. *Gravity.*

"I know, Jules told me. It's okay."

"She wants to talk about the school..."

He saw the worry in her face and felt his stomach tighten more. She was nearly as fearful as he was of Dan and Jules going away. Taking care of them had been her life for more than a decade, the sacred duty she had assumed on behalf of her beloved Maria Gambiari. Whenever she talked of the possibility of them leaving she would put her hands in the air with the fingers spread wide, as if to signify the emptiness.

"*No te preocupes. Todo estará bien.*" He said to her softly, soothing her with Spanish. *Don't worry, everything will be fine.* He should have it tattooed on his forehead for as many times a day as he uttered it.

Jules followed them both into the kitchen where Maria went back to her cooking as he sat at the table with cup of coffee and his laptop, checking for any new emails in the now eight-month battle for his family's soul.

He slapped the laptop closed as Juliana sat down next to him with a worried look. "Is there any news?"

"No news." He kissed her forehead. "*No te preocupes*. It will all work out." He said, not even convincing himself. Who knows, maybe Miranda would work her magic.

"Aren't you supposed to be at rehearsal soon?" Juliana was playing the summer with the Philharmonia Baroque orchestra.

"Yeah, but I was hoping you'd talk to grandma first."

"We're all having dinner tomorrow night at her house, so we'll talk then. Go get ready, I'll drop you off at rehearsal."

He called and met with Eleanor frequently to report on any events in her grandchildren's lives—performances, soccer games, school dances, report cards. *Keep your enemies close.* She was a devoted grandmother and an involved one. Once when she heard Danny was having problems in math, a fresh-faced Stanford grad student showed up at the door to tutor him through his geometry midterm. After Juliana's victory at a prestigious violin competition, Eleanor delivered a Stradivarius as a Christmas present, complete with a renowned Stanford music teacher to coach her on its intricacies. When they first brought it home, Will was so wracked with worry he had nightmares of someone carjacking them on their way to rehearsal or kidnapping Juliana at her music teacher's house. He begged her to wait until she was older to take possession of it, but she cherished it immediately, pleading with him to keep it. The instrument's sound was so suited to her, rich and honeyed, exquisitely nuanced, the low range of notes resonating in a way that physically reverberated through your body when she played. Even when she wasn't playing it, she would cradle it gently in her lap, plucking the strings or running the bow across it to tease out its dulcet tones.

"*Please* Will," she begged, "it gives so freely. It *sings*." In the end he didn't have the heart to keep it from her.

Eleanor Simpson Thompkins Ross was also a die-hard Stanford-alum and a generous benefactor of the college, which meant that every Christmas the entire Thompkins family was the recipient of the latest cardinal red Stanford gear, courtesy of a grateful endowment office. There were Stanford beer steins, Stanford sweatshirts, Stanford stadium blankets, backpacks, hats and pajamas.

"She knows we're a Cal family!" Will would lament to Lee, watching his children try on one after another sartorial slap in the face. "We're blood rivals!"

"Oh you take it way too seriously." Lee would laugh. "It's her little joke." Lee and Eleanor had always had an easy relationship that Will envied. "We get each other." Lee would say when Will asked him how he managed to stay so civil with her. Not that Will was complaining. His friend could sometimes be a secret weapon when he needed to call in reinforcements.

Will kissed Juliana goodbye and watched her walk off to the symphony hall, waiting to drive off until she was safely inside the doors. She looked back and waved through the glass, lifting the violin and smiling to show him they both were intact. He waved back and smiled. When he arrived back home he poured a scotch and allowed himself a moment to relax and think over the events of the last evening. It *had* been a great night with Miranda. Maybe she would be able to help Dave's case, but even if she couldn't, he felt a little less alone in the world.

In the middle of his thoughts, the door opened and Danny walked in. For an instant, when Will first saw him, he actually thought he was hallucinating.

"What *happened*?"

"It's a long story." The boy stood slumped in the hallway, his hair—matted and wet with sweat—was bright blue. One eye was purple and swollen shut, his clothes were covered in mud.

"Are you *OKAY*?" Will jumped out of his chair and scanned him up and down, his hands feeling his body for broken bones or internal injuries.

"I'm good, don't worry." Will examined his eye and jaw, both of them bruised and swelling bigger by the minute.

"Did you get beat up?"

"No, Rugby!" Dan said, a thrill still in his voice.

"Rugby?" Will asked, incredulous. "When did you start playing rugby?"

"Well it's kind of a long story."

"How about you tell it to me." He said sternly, staring at his bright blue hair. "Were you playing rugby with the Blue Man Group?"

"No, that's a whole *other* story."

"Let's hear it."

"Can I sit down, cause I'm kind of sore."

Will felt a twinge of sympathy. "Go sit on the couch. How about you start with the blue hair," he offered, exasperated.

"Okay, *that* wasn't actually my fault." Dan said, sinking into the cushions. "See, Morgan said semi-permanent meant you could wash it out."

"Semi-permanent …why were you dying your hair blue in the first place?"

"It's a long story."

"I know, you said that. Start talking."

"Okay, Well I was trying to switch up my look a little…"

"Mm hmn. What's her name?"

Dan slumped deeper. "Kelsey Garvey. She likes edgy guys, you know, like Simon Rosen, and this guy Billy French who has tattoos all over his neck and purple hair. So I figured there wasn't really time to get a tattoo or anything…plus you have to be 18."

"Wise choice." Will winced as he imagined his beautiful boy under the needle of some grimy, pot-smoking, tattoo artist.

"Yeah, so Morgan had the idea for blue hair."

"I'll be sure to thank him."

"I figured I could wash it out, 'cause it said *semi*-permanent, but then it came out *too* blue, you know, and I washed it about 10 times and nothing happened."

"Son, when you saw the word *permanent*, that should've been your first clue."

"Yeah."

"I know you were trying to impress this girl, but even if she likes the edgy look, you're not really a blue hair, edgy kind of guy. I mean, how much could you have in common?"

"Yeah. She's so cool though. I was just hoping…"

"So how did blue hair lead to a rugby game?"

"Okay, so I was walking back from Morgan's, and these guys over at the grad-school field were playing, and I was kind of bummed, you know, because of the whole blue hair thing, so I stopped to watch them play, and they asked me if I wanted to join in. It's such a cool sport, Will. They want me to join their team!"

"No."

"They only play after school—"

"NO."

"But they said I'm pretty good at it…"

"Babe, in your sterling athletic career you've had a broken arm, a smashed up knee, torn ligaments, a sprained ankle, bruised ribs, and more stitches than I can count. You're not playing rugby. I'm too old for you to take on another sport." The boy looked downcast, resigned to his fate.

"Am I grounded?"

Will let him twist for a minute. "No. I think walking around with blue hair for another month will be punishment enough. But you're definitely not going to your grandmother's tomorrow night for dinner, I've got enough to explain without you showing up with blue hair and a black eye."

"Sorry."

"Go wash up and help Maria with dinner." Dan dutifully got up and limped his way into the kitchen. Will listened for the sound of Maria's response when she saw him. In a few beats the Spanish started flying, loud and furious.

fifteen

The next morning, Will called Eleanor and told her he'd be coming to dinner, but without Dan and Jules. It wasn't just the black eye and blue hair. He decided it was time to go one-on-one with his grandmother, without the sensitivities of the kids getting in the way. He asked to bring Lee to provide an objective perspective as they talked out the situation, and he was relieved Eleanor agreed. The two of them headed to Oakhaven, Will with the usual knot in his chest.

"Never underestimate her." His father's words came back to haunt him.

"You have custody." Lee coached him. "You're a sterling parent. She can't override you. Everything that she's doing is strictly psychological, the key is not to let her get into your head."

Lee was right, why *was* he so worried? A suspicion had begun to work its way into Will's consciousness: What if Eleanor was *right*? What if Dan and Jules *would* be better off in Atherton, away from the chaos that their lives had become? Until now he hadn't allowed himself to consider that scenario, the thought of them leaving home filled him with such anxiety and dread. Even when they were away for short periods of time, on a school trip or with Eleanor on a vacation, he was miserable, feeling the phantom pain as though a limb had been cut off but was still cruelly sending its signals to the brain.

It was six o'clock when they arrived at Oakhaven's entrance gate. The sun was low in the sky and the soft light filtering through the trees gave everything a golden hue. Will buzzed the gate speaker and identified himself. The gate swung open slowly and they headed toward the house. The great oaks that lined the road rustled gently in the breeze, their trunks silvery in the early evening light. Lee became silent as the car made its way up to the circular driveway in front of the great stone house. Will could see his friend was falling under its spell, the same way Will had as a boy, before time and circumstances dispelled its magic. There was no denying the place's allure, especially now. It was an idyllic, pastoral world, far from prying detectives and the machinations of a scornful ex-wife. Jess took the car, and Eleanor opened the door to greet them.

"Can I get you a drink," She offered. Will had intended not to drink so he could keep his head clear, but the intimidating presence of his grandmother immediately changed his mind, so he opted for a scotch. Lee joined him.

"How are things at the house?" She asked, with genuine concern.

"About the same. Have you talked to Dave?"

"No, we don't talk. It's probably better that way, he wouldn't like what I have to say."

"He's feeling pretty bad about everything."

"I know, but it doesn't change what he's done. He brought hell down on this family and I'm not ready to let him off the hook. There are consequences." Will secretly agreed, but stayed silent. "I talked to Juliana yesterday, she seems worried. I feel bad about that. I don't want to disrupt their lives you know. I want to do what's best for them, no matter what you think."

"I don't think that...I know how much you love them," Will faltered. "I just...I'm not sure what the right thing to do is myself." His eyes drifted off exploring the familiar contours of the house. He looked outside the window at the pond where he and Dave raced their wooden boats, at the turquoise swimming pool and the gardens stretching as far as the eye could see. The serenity of it all began to soothe him. Why did he think of this place as enemy territory? It was still a cherished part of his childhood, filled with the memories of his parents and the joyful times they all spent here.

The three of them sat in the living room talking over the latest developments in Dave's case. He gazed up at the pastel seraphim looking down on him. Were they chastising him for not allowing his children to live here under their watchful eye in a state of eternal grace?

The brochure for Pembroke lay on the table in front of them. The photo showed a bucolic nest of buildings set in the gently sloping hills of Atherton, complete with exuberant images of teenagers—putting on a play, on an archaeological dig, playing in a string quartet, studying in a library filled with rare books. It was a world that appeared to be free of scull tattoos and lip piercings and blue hair, far from the rough and tumble of Berkeley High, rife with its urban distractions and perils, far from a scornful ex-wife. What right did he have to keep his children from this privileged life?

He sat silently, listening to Lee questioning Eleanor about the pros and cons of moving the kids. He admired his friend for keeping his focus on the task at hand; he was losing his by the minute. He tried to imagine what his father's advice would be. *"We want them to stay here in Berkeley."* But his father couldn't have foreseen the complications his second son would bring into the equation, and worse, how the loss of Henry Thompkins' own wise and steady hand at the tiller of the household would change everything. How could his father ever have expected Will to take his place raising Dan and Jules? He was dropped into parenthood like a goldfish in a pond, without any time to acclimate to his new environment. And now…his next move would be the most crucial one in all of their lives. The world Henry Thompkins' children would enter for the coming years would shape them as adults. Their friends, their social circles, their intellectual future would all be carved out by life at Oakhaven and at Pembroke, and it was a universe away from Berkeley. It was the road not taken.

They ate dinner civilly and talked some more, until there was nothing more to talk about. They agreed to engage Dan and Jules in the real prospect of moving to their grandmother's house. They would visit the school, take a tour, talk it out with Pembroke's academic counselor. After that they would decide.

The mood on the drive home was somber, both men deep in thought. "So, what are you thinking?" Lee finally broke the silence.

Will paused for a long minute. "I'm thinking, 'Check.'"

Lee didn't answer. The thought of his own life without Dan and Jules was difficult to conceive—a world without them walking through his door full of stories about their day or needing advice about their brother, spending the night when Will had to work late, recitals, soccer games, countless evenings spent around the big redwood table, talking and feasting on Maria's cooking. Together they had become a little universe of their own, his universe. He couldn't imagine how he would function in the vacuum that would be left in their absence.

When they arrived home to Avalon Street it was dark. Will pulled the car into the driveway and saw a small flash of light come from a car across the street. A reporter. Lee shot out of the car, incensed. He marched across the street and engaged in a heated exchange. By the time Will got out of the car to intervene, it was too late. Lee had already grabbed the camera through the window, smashed it to the ground and handed it back to the hapless reporter, punctuated with obscenities. The car screeched off down the street.

Will looked at his friend. "That can't be good."

"He caught me at a bad time." A slow grin began to break across Lee's face. "Nice camera though."

"Past tense." Will grinned back.

"Yeah. I might look into getting one of those."

The next month unfolded with no change in Dave's circumstances, if anything things got nastier. Everyone began to be resigned to their fate. Dan and Jules visited Pembroke with their grandmother and Will. They were given a tour of the campus by a gaggle of charming students and met with the Head of School, a pleasant woman who was clearly excited to add Eleanor's bright and well-connected grandchildren to her stable. They were all skilled promoters, and they had a lot of capital to work with. It was a gorgeous campus, with every educational resource money could buy—expertly outfitted science labs, computer labs, sports fields, music rooms. There was a digital animation and film studio that looked like it belonged at Lucas Ranch, captivating Dan, who was already showing a gift for shooting and editing film. Juliana was enthralled by the mini orchestra hall and its cache of rare instruments which could be borrowed at will, including a Vuillaume violin that she stared at lovingly in its locked glass case. At 60,000 dollars a year per student no resource went un-gilded. As they toured, Will found himself impressed but taciturn. He knew his father would have been critical of the exclusivity of it all. This was a place for the very blessed…and very rich. Three years at Pembroke would turn his children into something different than what Henry Thompkins had envisioned for them in Berkeley.

In the meantime, Will tried to navigate the upheaval in his household. They talked nightly about the pluses and minuses of going. Dan and Jules, with youthful confidence, had elaborate logistical plans to keep both worlds intact—having Harry drive them wildly back and forth from place to place—to lessons, friends' houses, rehearsals, soccer, school. Will listened patiently, knowing in his bones that they were slipping away from him. One weekend away from home would skip to two, and then a month, and before long he would be a casual observer in his children's lives, their daily rhythms, which had been as familiar as his own heartbeat, would be lost to him. The thought filled him with nausea and dread.

To add to his worry, he was concerned about Maria, her own routine thrown into upheaval. She was desolate at the idea they would be gone all week. She normally went to Margarita's on the weekends, but now that Dan and Jules insisted they would spend weekends at home in Berkeley, she didn't want to leave them. She fretted over their schedule. She kept herself busy by tidying their rooms, arranging and rearranging things they might need. Even Lee started finding excuses to miss dinner, the pain of the conversation becoming too much for him. As the weeks wore on, everyone tiptoed around the elephant in the room, trying to be upbeat, but the atmosphere in the house was strained. They were now scheduled to move in September for the Fall semester. As summer faded, everyone's mood darkened.

Will was sitting at his usual spot at the kitchen table finishing his coffee when the doorbell rang. He never knew who would be on the other side these days, so he approached it with dread. It was FedEx with a box for him. He signed for it and glanced into the street to see who might be lying in wait. Curiously, it was empty. No reporters or PIs lurking. Thank god. Maybe they would have a reprieve for the weekend. He walked inside and plopped the package on the kitchen table to get another cup of coffee. He stared at the narrow, elongated box—more papers from the lawyer. He pulled the tab and sprung it open. Inside was a stack of legal papers tied with a thick red silk ribbon, some poisonous new missive from Heather no doubt.

He started to flip through them nervously, reading the text. It was the house deed. His heart began to pound. He pored over it until he got to the names: William Henry Thompkins, David Thaddeus Thompkins, Juliana Maria Thompkins, Daniel Douglas Thompkins—no mention of Heather! He pulled the ribbon off the rest of the thick stack and began to read furiously. It was a copy of the divorce settlement, all of it, signed and notarized, *Heather Eloise Hopkins*. Next to it was an empty line for Dave's signature. Will's heart was banging as he scanned through the document. He found the list of possessions and settlement funds…*Nothing* about the house. In fact, there was not much of anything, no listing of Dave's inheritance, his 401K, or even his condo in Marin. Will got to the bottom of the stack and found a single sheet of creamy vellum paper. On it was a note, written in longhand.

It said, "*Love, Miranda.*"

sixteen

I t was poker night, and Will arrived early to help Lee set up.

"Where's Dave? I thought he was coming early so he could visit with the kids?"

"He left a message. His surgery ran late."

"Oh, *right*. You mean the surgery he was performing on that new woman he's seeing."

"Alexa seems very nice to me. Just because you don't have a social life, doesn't mean you have to be bitter about his."

"I'd have a social life too if I wasn't raising two teenagers by myself."

"No you wouldn't."

It had been more than a year since Will's custody brush with Eleanor, and to Lee's frustration the experience had only redoubled Will's efforts to commandeer every aspect of his children's lives at the expense of his own. It was now his holy crusade.

"What's that supposed to mean?"

"Think about it."

"I'm a responsible parent, okay? I take my duties seriously."

"If by that you mean you're a control freak, then yes, you're a responsible parent. On that subject, the kids came to me and asked if I would talk to you about not chaperoning on the New York field trip next month."

"Seriously? "I *always* chaperone on field trips..."

"I know, that's why they don't want you to go this time."

"Why?"

"Because they're sixteen, they want a little independence."

"Did they say that?"

"Yes."

"Did they specifically say I was cramping their style?"

"Yes."

"Wow...that hurts."

They're *sixteen* Will, try to remember what that was like. You don't want your dad along on a field trip when you're sixteen."

"But we do everything together."

"That's the problem. They need a little space."

"Wow. I'm stunned. I don't know what to say..."

"Say you'll let them go alone this time."

"But we've never been apart like that. You know I'm not good with them going off on their own."

"You sent them off with Eleanor to Tahiti last year." Lee was referring to the two-week luxury cruise through the Pacific islands with their grandmother, Eleanor's consolation prize for Dan and Jules not coming to live at Oakhaven.

"That's different, that was just a forward pass, you know, with protection. This is like…a Hail Mary."

"They're going to go off to college before you know it, you might as well get used to the idea of them being on their own."

"To *Berkeley*."

"How do you know they'll go to Cal? Maybe they won't get in, maybe they'll want to go somewhere else."

Will grimaced. "Are you trying to stress me out on purpose?"

Lee threw up his hands in exasperation. "See, this is what I mean."

Will went silent.

"What ever happened to that radiologist you were dating?" Lee probed.

"I don't know, it didn't work out. We had too much in common."

"Excuse me?"

"You know, medicine, the hospital, patients, everything we did was so similar, it's like dating your sister."

Lee rolled his eyes. "So…with the attorney you didn't have enough in common, with the doctor you have too much in common. And you wonder why you have no social life?"

"I'm trying."

"No you're not."

Will was still sulking when Seth and Mike came through the front door without knocking, grabbing a beer and settling in at the card table.

"Is this an inconvenient time, ladies?" Mike said, noting the thick silence.

"Lee was just lecturing me on my dating life."

"Ah. Any movement with the radiologist?"

"No, they have too much in common." Lee said sarcastically.

"Can we talk about something besides my love life for a change?" Will pleaded.

Lee sat down and started dealing the cards.

"How are the kids?" Mike asked, attempting to break the tension.

"Sore subject." Lee slapped the deck down in the middle of the table. "They're growing up."

"They're great." Will countered. "How about Josh?" Well he passed biology, thank god. All he has to do is get through Spring semester and he'll be off to Spelman. Right now he's a pain in the ass—cocky, staying out late, flirting with girls, thinks he's Mr. Cool, I could kill him."

"You just described every 17-year old boy in Berkeley." Will tossed in his bet. "You're such a big talker, every time I see you with that kid you're giving him big bear hugs. You're going to miss him and you know it."

"Yeah. I'm going to miss him." Mike leaned back in his chair. "I just can't stand living with him."

"Is Juliana playing with Philharmonia this Fall?" Seth asked. "I bought a season's ticket."

"Yeah, she's playing four concerts."

"I decided when I get married I'm going to have her play at my wedding. I already asked her, she said she would."

All three men stared at him.

"What? You don't think I'm going to get married?" Seth looked wounded.

"You're going to have to start being a whole lot less picky before that is going to happen, my friend. There is no perfect woman out there, trust me, I'm married."

"I'm not looking for the perfect woman." Seth protested

"Yes you are," They said in unison.

"What was wrong with that last one, the blonde elementary school teacher?" Lee probed.

"The vegan?"

"What's wrong with being a vegan—this is Berkeley, half the women here are vegans."

"She was too pure. I found myself sneaking hamburgers from Oscar's and then brushing my teeth so she didn't smell the meat. Not to mention the way she looked at my leather shoes, you'd think I was walking on puppies."

"How about the one before that, the architect?" Will queried.

"Too intellectual. It was like dating your philosophy professor. She felt she had to comment on the cultural significance of every building we ever set foot in. I had to go to the library before every date to bone up. It was exhausting. I'm not that smart."

"And what about the one with the cats?" Mike teased.

"Three cats? That's a recipe for disaster. In five years it'll be 12 cats and she'll be knitting little jackets for them. No, I stand by the cat lady decision. I'm a dog person. Give me a big dumb Lab any time."

"Maybe that's what you should look for in a woman." Mike offered. Now they were all laughing hard. Will was grateful to have the attention focused on someone else for a change.

seventeen

D
r. Thompkins, I have a 34-year old female with appendicitis in room four. I think she needs surgery, but she has an arrhythmia, I'm not sure what to do--should I call cardiology?" Will was overseeing the interns, standing in for his chief resident who had just gotten word his wife went into labor. He liked to stay connected to life in the trenches, to teach younger doctors and take a break from his bloodless daily bureaucratic duties.

"Vitals?"

"Blood pressure is 185 over 98, pulse is 170, fever is 102."

"Did the labs come back yet?"

"Yeah, here they are." The intern handed the file over to Will nervously. "Her white count is pretty high. She has guarding, rebound pain in the lower right quadrant. Onset is two days. I can't hear any peristalsis."

"Do you have her hooked to a monitor?"

"Not yet."

"Get her hooked up now. Call cardiology and have them send someone down. With this white count and fever she may already be septic. Notify surgery." Will headed for the examining room, the intern still in tow.

"Her name is Samantha Parrish, She's a professor at Cal."

"Okay, I've got it." Will walked into the room to see a woman curled up on the gurney. She was pale and damp with fever and obviously in a lot of pain. Another woman, presumably her friend, was by her side trying to comfort her.

"Hello Ms. Parrish, I'm Dr. Thompkins."

"Finally, a grownup." The friend said, exasperated.

The intern was still at Will's heels. "You're done. OUT." Will said. The intern scuttled out the door trying to evaporate.

"How are you doing?" Will's voice became gentle. The woman uncoiled from her misery long enough to look up at him.

"Besides the excruciating pain and nausea, I was planning to go salsa dancing."

Will smiled. Even wracked with pain she had an endearing face. She had soft blue eyes, and her reddish blond hair had been hurriedly tied up in a disheveled knot and was sticking out crazily. "Well, before you do, is it okay if I check you out?"

"Someone already did," she waved her hand toward the evaporated intern.

"Yeah, that was my intern. He's one of my best, but between you and me I don't trust him farther than I can throw him."

He saw her smile, and almost imperceptibly her body relaxed slightly onto the gurney. He put his stethoscope to her heart to listen for the arrhythmia.

"It's not my heart, it's my appendix I think."

"I know. I just want to listen for a minute, okay?"

"It *really* hurts..."

"We're going to get you something for the pain in a minute, as soon as we get this all sorted out, okay?"

"Okay."

"So shhh. Let me listen, all right?"

"I was just trying to help you get to the point."

Will put the stethoscope back to her chest; he could hear the arrhythmia clearly, it was nasty.

"Do you have a history of heart problems?"

"Goodness no. I come from very hardy stock. I'm from Maine."

"I see." The monitor arrived and he placed the clip onto her finger. The screen registered what he had already heard. It was Wolfe Parkinson complicated by atrial fibrillation, no doubt made worse by the infection and fever. She was in some trouble.

"I'm just going to examine your abdomen, okay? Tell me from one to ten how bad the pain is." He pressed gently, circling in closer to her appendix.

"Ten, ten, TEN!" she yelled out. Her friend glared at him. "Can you get her something for the *pain*?"

Will nodded. "Ms. Parrish you have acute appendicitis. We need to get you into surgery as soon as possible to get it taken care of. You also have an irregular heartbeat, so a cardiologist is going to check you out before you go in. Sound okay?"

"Okay."

"Good. We're going to have you sign some papers and then get you something for the pain."

Will saw her start to cry softly.

"Don't worry." He squeezed her arm. "We're going to get you all fixed up…you'll be out salsa dancing in no time." She managed a weak smile then turned suddenly pale and reached her arm out unsuccessfully for the blue plastic dish by her bed to throw up, the bulk splashing onto Will.

"Oh, sorry…so sorry." She laid back down, even more miserable.

"No worries, it happens all the time." Will casually wiped the vomit off his scrubs. After years in the ER and two kids he was unfazed by any bodily fluids that came flying at him. He turned to her friend. "I'm going to to arrange for a surgeon and get her prepped. Are you going to stay with her?

"Yes, I'll be right here."

"Good. There are some consent papers to sign, they'll be in here in a minute with them. Then we'll get her something for the pain…. is there a husband we should call, or significant other?"

"No. I'm taking care of her," the woman said protectively, holding her friend's hand tightly.

"Okay then, they'll tell you where to wait while she goes into surgery." Will looked back one last time at Samantha Parrish curled up in pain on the gurney, her blue eyes blinking back tears. She looked so vulnerable lying there, waiting for someone to relieve her misery. Even though he'd seen the same look a thousand times in patients, he never got immune to it. "Don't worry," He said gently, squeezing her arm again, "Everything's going to be fine."

He left the room and found Carlotta. "The patient in 4, Parrish, is an appy with a pretty severe case of Wolfe Parkinson and an atrial flutter, we need to have cardiology consult with the surgeon and anesthesiologist, I don't want her going in there without them aware of what's going on. Get an EKG and get a drip on her, she may be septic and she's in a lot of pain, so we don't have much time." He finished making his notes on her chart and emailed it to Carlotta, then walked to surgery to look for Ira Feinberg, the head surgeon. "Ira, I have an appy with complications coming your way, can you take it…?"

"I'm taking it, Carlotta already told me. I called Seth, he's coming down."

"It's a pretty nasty arrhythmia …"

"I know, I saw the EKG. We'll keep an eye on it."

"Hey." Lee plopped himself down at their usual table in the cafeteria. "Is it me, or is it crazy in here today. I've had patients lined up since 8:00 this morning. It's like a full moon or something."

"Yeah, it's like that in the ER too, we've been slammed all morning. Listen, I met the most fantastic woman…"

"Really?" Lee was always interested in Will's attempts to resuscitate his love life.

"Yeah, I don't even know how to describe her. She has blue eyes and this reddish blond hair that she wears up, and it kind of sticks out in places, she's beautiful...and she's funny, she totally blew me away."

"Did you ask her out?"

"Well, it's awkward—Ira is doing an appendectomy on her right now."

"She's a *patient*?"

"Yeah."

"*Your* patient?"

"Yeah." I'm covering for Matt. She came in with appendicitis this morning.

"I see. So, I'm curious, what were her symptoms?"

"The usual...rebound pain, guarding, vomiting, high fever..."

"So she was vomiting and she had a high fever and she was funny?"

"Yeah. It's hard to explain, you know."

"No, I have to say, I don't. I've never fallen in love with a patient who came in vomiting with a fever who was on her way into surgery."

"I feel like we had something, there was like an energy between us."

"Really? When you were feeling her up to confirm the appy diagnosis, or when she was vomiting?"

"Well it's not like she was vomiting the whole time, it was just the once."

"So how do you know she's available?"

"I asked her girlfriend who brought her in. It was a little awkward."

"You asked her friend if she was single while she was having an appendicitis attack?"

"I didn't do it like *that*, give me some credit. I asked if there was a husband or significant other we should call."

"So how do you know the girlfriend wasn't her lesbian partner? This *is* Berkeley you know."

"Nah, I didn't get that vibe. The girlfriend did seem a little put off, but not in a jealous lesbian partner way, more in a 'protecting my girlfriend' way."

"Seems like you've gotten very good at picking up the subtleties of women all of a sudden."

"I can't explain it, I just know."

"So what's next—are you going to visit her in recovery and ask her out?"

"Of *course* not. But I need to get Ira to agree not to release her too soon. I want time to talk to her before she goes home. I don't know, I feel like I shouldn't lose her."

"Wow, you're really smitten."

"I am."

"Well I'm sure Ira will bend hospital protocol to satisfy your dating needs—what are friends for?"

"Well I was thinking, she has an arrhythmia and pretty high blood pressure, Seth is consulting, he'll probably want to keep her an extra day to make sure she's stabilized. "

"So she was *hypertensive*, vomiting, high fever, in pain and still funny...?"

"And smart. You know how I love smart women."

"*And* beautiful—in an appendicitis-hair-sticking-out kind of way."

"Yes."

"You are a crazy man, you know that? Gorgeous women at this hospital throw themselves at you all the time and you're never interested, but you fall head over heals for a complete stranger incapacitated by appendicitis."

"I'm telling you, if you met this woman you would know what I mean, she's amazing. I've got to go. I have to find out if she's out of recovery and talk to Ira."

"Good luck."

"Thanks, I'll need it. I can't eat, finish my lunch."

"I intend to." Lee said, reaching across the table and plucking the uneaten sandwich from Will's plate.

Will was standing at the side of Samantha Parrish's bed reading her heart monitor when she woke up, blurry eyed.

"Hi there..."

"Where am I?" She blinked her eyes trying to focus in on her surroundings.

"You're in the hospital—you had appendicitis and you had surgery."

She looked up at the IV apparatus, tracing the tube down to her wrist, and closed her eyes again.

"How are you feeling?"

"Seriously high."

"That would be the drugs." She turned toward him to look at his face and winced from the pain of moving. "The surgery went well, your appendix is gone, you're all fixed up. Dr. Feinberg will explain everything, he's stopping by later." He looked into her eyes and found himself looking away in embarrassment. They only met once, but somehow she felt so intimate to him. He was afraid she could read what was in his mind.

"You do have a heart condition, I mentioned it before, an arrhythmia called Wolfe-Parkinson White." He was trying to keep the conversation professional, but his eyes returned to her face, following the contours of it, trying to take in what it was that made her so disarming. "The cardiologist will talk to you about it. We were a little concerned about it in surgery, but you came through just fine.

"A heart condition?

"Yes. An arrhythmia."

"Are you sure?"

"I'm sure."

"I'm from very hardy stock..."

"So you said. Unfortunately, being from Maine doesn't prevent you from having a heart condition. You can see it here." He pointed to the monitor, where the rhythmic fluctuations of her heart were playing out on the screen. "See this big peak here, and this slurred upstroke," he explained as she tried to focus her bleary eyes on the monitor. That's a delta wave—see how short this interval is? And this here," he pointed to a scribble of rapid beats, "is atrial fibrillation, see how fast and disorganized it is?"

"I see." She sighed and closed her eyes, the pain over-whelming her. He looked away from the monitor to her face, allowing himself to take in her features now that her eyes were closed. She was so…endearing, even in her present state of post-surgery distress. She began to drift back into sleep again and he remembered why he was there, Ira asked him to check on her before he got out of his last surgery.

"Okay if I check your incision?" He asked softly, pulling her back from her slumber. She opened her eyes again.

"I'm in no position to stop you." He pulled the covers back and gently checked the wound. Her body was limp and pale from the trauma of surgery and anesthesia. She was feverish. He put the stethoscope to her abdomen and then to her heart to listen to the patterns that were playing on the screen. When he finished, he adjusted the blanket to cover her. She moaned from misery. She looked at him as if asking for help.

"Did you know you have pain medication right here?" He showed her the morphine drip next to her bed. "All you have to do is squeeze it. It'll give just the right amount."

She fumbled with the pump and he helped her by put-ting his hand over hers to guide it to the valve. The touch of his palm on her soft skin sent a wave of electricity through him. She pushed the valve and he saw the drug go into her. "You should feel that pretty quickly," he said, hoping to comfort her.

"Thank you."

"You're welcome." She drifted off again and then woke with a start.

"Did I throw up on you?"

"Well...*near* me, not totally on me. No worries, it happens all the time. I have that effect on patients." He smiled.

"Sorry..."

"Not a problem at all," he looked at her face, it was pained, but expressive, sentient in spite of the drugs.

"You have a very nice face," she said, as if she knew he was reading hers.

"That's the morphine talking."

"But...worried eyes." She peered into them. "You're a worrier, aren't you." He shifted uneasily on his feet.

"I have been known to worry occasionally..."

"Oh—" Her eyes suddenly pooled with empathy. She reached out and touched her hand to his cheek. "I see pain in there...I'm sorry." Will was taken aback. He saw her close her eyes again, the morphine pulling her deeper down as it took hold. He focused his eyes on the monitor, trying to regain his composure, watching the rhythms of her heart on the screen. What did she mean she could see pain in his eyes? *He wasn't in pain.* He had a good life, wonderful children, friends, a great career. He had put the pain of losing his parents behind him years ago. He was *happy*. His eyes went from the monitor back to her face. Her hair was still sticking out in a crazy knot. The hospital gown was pulled back where the heart monitor lines were attached, revealing the soft curve of her neck and collar bone. She looked so vulnerable. He wanted to find a reason to stay longer, but he didn't have one. She was asleep. He took one last look at her and headed down the stairs to his office, unnerved by what had happened. As he did, he ran into Carlotta.

"Where have you been? The residents have been looking for you, you were supposed to do rounds with them."

"I went up to check on the appy patient from this morning." Carlotta sniffed something.

She scanned his face. "Oh my god. You have fallen for a patient."

"Don't be ridiculous." *How did she know these things? Was his face open reading for every woman?*

"Do you want me to find out her status?"

"*No.*" He tried to sound indifferent, avoiding eye contact. "*maybe...*"

"I'll see what I can do." She disappeared down the hallway.

He went back to his office, but he couldn't concentrate on work so he got a cup of coffee and walked the halls. It was late at night, usually his favorite time at the hospital, but tonight he was restless. It had been a long time since he'd been so attracted to a woman, and never like this. It was unsettling. He was startled by Carlotta standing in front of him, returning from her mission. *How long had he been walking?*

"Not that you're interested, but I have the scoop on the professor." They were locked in a stare-down, each one waiting for the other to break.

"*AND...?*" Will finally gave in.

Carlotta looked victorious. "She's not attached. She just came out of a bad break-up three months ago—an attorney at the university, he was cheating on her."

"Geeze Carlotta, how do you do that?"

"I'm a *nurse*. And by the way, she's had lots of attractive male visitors, so you better make your move soon," she said, heading back down the hallway.

"I'M NOT 'MAKING A MOVE!'" he called out after her, but she had already disappeared into her office.

Who would cheat on that incredible woman? And why did he care so much?

As the night wore on he began to convince himself the best thing to do was to walk away from her. Nothing good could come out of a relationship that made him feel so unsteady on his feet. *Why was he even calling it a relationship? He just met her!* He would not go back and see her, Ira and Seth were on the case now, she would be well taken care of. He had enough going on in his life with his kids and the hospital, he didn't need a woman like that to complicate things. He grabbed his laptop and keys and was heading for the car when his cell went off.

"Will, It's Ira, are you still at the hospital?"

"Yeah, what's up?"

"Can you go see the appy patient from this morning— Samantha Parrish? Her fever is spiking. Terry is supposed to be on call for the floor but she's not answering. I'm stuck here at my kid's play. Her BP is high and the arrhythmia isn't responding to the medication. I called Seth, we ordered blood work and new meds, but I'd feel better if you could check her out in person to see what's going on." Will felt his stomach tighten at the thought of seeing her again.

"Okay, I'll go up now."

"Thanks buddy. Rachel will kill me if I leave here before it's over."

"No problem. How's the play?"

"Fiddler on the Roof for 8-year olds. It's high theatre."

"I've been there, my friend, *many* times."

"I know. I have more sympathy for you now."

"How is Noah doing?"

"Fine, he makes a great villager. I recommend he doesn't quit his day job."

Will laughed. "Wise advice."

"I better go back in, text me to let me know how she is."

"Will do." When he walked into the room, Samantha Parrish was asleep. The monitor that registered the rhythms of her heart was beeping manically. Her blood pressure was too high, and the a-fib, even more pronounced, was bouncing crazily across the screen in rapid, erratic patterns. The floor nurse was attaching new meds to the IV. Will looked at the chart to see if any blood work was back and what new medications Ira prescribed. "When did her fever shoot up?"

"About an hour ago, right after you left. Her arrhythmia isn't responding to the drugs."

"Hopefully the new meds will help." He looked around the room, for the first time he noticed it was filled with flower arrangements.

"She's a pretty popular professor, there've been students coming and going all day."

"Yeah, I see that. Let's try to keep everyone out for the next 24 hours 'till we know where this is going."

"Okay, I'll let them know at the front desk." He stood at the side of the bed and watched the monitor for a few minutes to look for signs of danger in the rhythms.

"Do you want me to stay?" the nurse asked.

"No, thanks. I'm going to check her out and sit here for awhile to see how things go."

He checked her wound and listened to her abdomen and lungs for any sign of trouble, but there wasn't anything alarming. If the fever subsided soon they could assume it was just a post-op reaction and not a sign of an undetected infection or something more sinister. In the mean time they had to deal with the arrhythmia.

He dimmed the light above her to keep it out of her eyes and pulled up a chair next to the bed to sit it out for a while, hoping the new heart meds would take hold. His eyes traced the lines of her face. It was flushed with fever and he could see she was in pain. She had probably forgotten to use the morphine pump. She stirred, and the pain woke her up. She opened her eyes to see Will sitting there.

"You again..."

"Yes, can't get rid of me." He smiled.

"It's so hot."

"Your fever's up, but we've got you on some new antibiotics, they should help soon."

She winced with pain. "Did you take your pain medication? She shook her head.

"Forgot."

"That incision is bound to be hurting right about now. Need some help?" She nodded, and he reached over and squeezed the medication into her arm. "That should work pretty fast."

"Thank you." She smiled at him as the morphine began to take hold.

"You're welcome. You have quite a fan club here." He motioned to the flowers filling the room.

"My freshman. Like newly hatched chicks and I'm the first face they see."

He laughed. "Yeah, kind of like my interns, except mostly they run the other direction when they see me."

She looked into his eyes. "No, you seem kind."

"Well, to my patients, not so much to my interns. But I'm not trying to be popular I'm trying to make them good doctors."

"I just want to be popular." A slow smile came across her face.

"Really Professor Parrish? Well that is an interesting side of you. I'll have to note it in your chart."

She was so lovely when she smiled. He felt himself being pulled in again.

"Why aren't you with your wife? The nurses said you had a play..."

"Oh, no. I'm not married, that's Ira—Dr. Feinberg. His eight-year old Noah is in a play tonight. I'm filling in for him."

"Oh." She closed her eyes, waiting for the pain to subside. He watched her, the quiet between them broken only by the soft sounds of her breathing. A few more minutes passed and she broke the silence. "Do you have family in Berkeley?"

"I do. I'm a fourth generation Berkeleyan."

"Aren't you lucky to be from this place."

"I never thought of it that way, but I guess I am."

"I'm from Boothbay, Maine, third generation."

"Maine is beautiful country. Do you still have family there?"

"My mom. My father died when I was young. He was a doctor too."

"I lost my parents 15 years ago, but I have three siblings here." *Why did he tell her that?* She fixed her eyes on him. He was afraid she could see through him, but her face was so disarming he couldn't look away.

"Are you close to them?"

"I am."

"I'm an only child." She looked around the room taking in the surroundings and became suddenly pensive. He saw a sadness flicker cross her face, as if her thoughts were darkening. "It's awfully easy to be hard-boiled about everything in the daytime, but at night it's another thing." She said, closing her eyes again as if to shut out the melancholy. He wondered if she was referring to the cheating attorney.

"Sorry, can't remember who wrote that...Hemingway I think."

"No apology necessary," Will said gently. He didn't want their conversation to end, but he could see the morphine and exhaustion were taking hold. He sat back in the chair and watched the heart monitor for signs that the meds were starting to work. Her blood pressure had dropped a little, but the arrhythmia was still going strong. He decided to wait it out longer. If it didn't improve he would call Seth. He settled in and watched her as she slept. She was peaceful now, the pain was subsiding. Her hair was loose, freshly brushed, probably by the nurses. Wisps of it framed her face and spread out against the pillow. He tried to imagine what she was like when she was well, fully animated, teaching her class. Once again he was overcome by a feeling that he didn't want to lose her. He was lost in thought when Seth came into the room.

"Hey, I didn't know you were coming..."

"Ira called me, I wanted to check on her. Is she responding to the new meds?"

"Not much, it's been about an hour."

Seth watched the monitor intently for a minute and put the stethoscope to her heart to listen. "Why don't you go home. I think the drugs are beginning to take hold, but I'm going to wait it out for awhile just to be safe."

"Okay. Will you give me a call and let me know how it goes?"

"Yeah. I'll let Ira know too."

"Okay, I'll head out then." Will took one last look at Samantha Parrish and left the room. He headed down the dark hallway, its lights dimmed for the night, and out into the parking lot, where the fluorescent lamps glared off of the scattering of cars that were still left there. He turned the key and started the car for his short drive back home. How many times had he made the same drive between his two worlds—Avalon Street and Mercy Hospital? They were only a few miles apart, and the avenues and shops, the restaurants, schools and ball fields nestled inside those worlds constituted the contracted galaxy that he had lived in for most of his life. That had been okay with him up until now. But tonight, as he travelled the familiar winding streets home to the beloved house that had been his great-great grandfather's and his father's, Will Thompkins felt lonely.

For the next four days, as Samantha Parrish healed, Will found himself pulled to a nightly ritual of visiting her. They would talk late into the evening, the conversation flowing easily between them—their experiences growing up, grad school, Berkeley. She described making her way from her provincial town in Maine to the University of Washington to teach English Literature, and her thrill at being recruited by Cal. She told him about her passion for Berkeley—its rich intellectual life, its bohemian spirit and open-mindedness, the beauty of its architecture—the Arts and Crafts houses with their exposed beamed ceilings and stone fireplaces. She'd researched and visited every Bernard Maybeck and Julia Morgan building in the city. Sometimes, when it was a private residence, she would stand on the sidewalk outside trying to imagine what life was like inside. Nearly every Saturday, rain or shine, she began her day by traversing Maybeck's Rose Walk, the charmed set of winding steps linking Euclid Avenue to Rose Street. She rambled the crooked streets beneath the Claremont Hotel, the grand, white turn-of-the-century chateau that held dominion over the east hills of Berkeley, including Will's own house on Avalon. She loved Berkeley in the summer—the Botanical Gardens, huddled in Strawberry Canyon just up the hill from her office—blooming in green and pink and lavender, the bustling 'gourmet ghetto' with its cheese shops, bakeries and farmer's markets, its tiny patches of lawn filled with students, their lunches spread out, taking in the sun. She even loved it in the winter, when the damp and chill settled into the campus, driving everyone into the warm glow of the libraries, cafes and coffee shops.

As she shared her affection for the world in which Will had grown up, the world he had reveled in as a boy, he began to see it with fresh eyes. He had become so consumed by the hospital and obligations—and grief—that the luminescence of Berkeley had dimmed in the years since his parents' death. He'd gone to football and basketball games, and given generously to the alumni association, but Samantha Parrish was rekindling his own memories of the charmed galaxy in which they all orbited.

Each time they talked Will unearthed more of his own recollections of growing up in Berkeley, and of his father's deep love of the place. He told Samantha how as a young history professor Henry Thompkins had met his intellectual hero, John Kenneth Galbraith. Years later he regaled Will with tales of Galbraith's own reverence for Berkeley: "The beauty, but also the built-in dissonance, the will to be inconvenient, to question official wisdom—" Henry Thompkins would quote the scholar from memory, trying to impress upon his son the rarified nature of their little universe. He related to Will with pride that in Galbraith's Cambridge study above his desk, amid pictures of him with presidents and prime ministers, was a blue-and-gold pennant advertising his enduring love for Cal. Berkeley was Galbraith's 'true north,' his father told Will, and remained so until he died. Henry Thompkins loved to tell that story because Berkeley had been his own true north as well.

After Will left her room that particular night, his mind flush with fresh memories of his father, he heard a ping on his hospital email. It was from the nurses' station, via Samantha Parrish's laptop:

"I strolled across the California campus—over Strawberry Creek, by the Campanile, down by the Library, out Sather Gate. I was taught, as were most of my generation, that no one should allow himself the weak luxury of sentiment or even emotion…I was suddenly overwhelmed by the thought that I loved this place—the paths, trees, flowers, buildings…I was deeply embarrassed." —*John Kenneth Galbraith*

The note was signed simply, 'Samantha.'

A few days later Samantha Parrish was sitting dressed on the edge of the hospital bed ready to go home. Will anxiously rounded the corner to her room one last time. She smiled broadly when she saw him in the doorway.

"So you're getting out of here." He said.

"Yup, I'm getting out."

"Ira let you go."

"Yes." She grinned.

I'm going to have speak to him about that, I won't like this place as much without you."

"Thank you for everything, I enjoyed all our bedside chats."

"Me too." He shifted self-consciously on his feet. "Do you have a ride? You're not going to drive yourself I hope. I wouldn't put it past you."

"My friend Meg is getting the car."

"Good. Promise me you're going to take care of yourself, have that heart followed up on."

"I Promise."

"And just lay around for a week or two, let those grad students do all the work."

"Got it, be lazy, I'll try." And you...try not to worry so much." She fixed her soft blue eyes on him and he felt himself falling.

"I'll try."

The wheelchair arrived and Will took it from the volunteer. "I'll take you down." He rolled the chair into the elevator and leaned against the wall facing her, working up his nerve.

"So now that you're officially discharged, and before you go out into that other world that I'm not a part of, I was wondering if you'd like to have dinner some time...I wont mind if you'd rather forget everything about this experience and say no, I would completely understand."

"No." she was flustered. "I mean, no I *don't* want to forget you, yes I'd love to have dinner some time, I was hoping you'd ask."

"That's great!" He was embarrassed by his own enthusiasm. Then he saw her face light up in the way he had come to look forward to. "Maybe in a week or two, when you're feeling up to it?"

"That's a deal." She fished in her purse and scribbled her phone number on a piece of paper and handed it to him. Her friend's car drove up, and as he helped settle her into the car seat, the fragrance of her freshly showered skin drifted up to him tantalizingly. He closed the door and watched as the car disappeared down the street into the maze of neighborhood houses and shops. She was gone into the world outside, but now he had an invisible cord connecting himself to her so she wouldn't be lost. He walked back into the hospital, holding the piece of paper tight in his hand.

"Well…did you ask her?" Lee sat across from Will at their usual table, grilling him.

"Yes."

"Did she accept?"

"Yes. She said she was hoping I would ask." Lee slapped Will's hand in a high-five.

"I'm telling you I'm intoxicated with that woman, she's…I don't know. There's *something*."

"Well good for you, you're taking a leap. And it's not a boring radiologist or a ballbusting attorney, it's a real date. I'm proud of you."

"I know, she's amazing…I hope she doesn't change her mind."

"Don't start sabotaging your joy so soon, okay?

"Okay."

eighteen

A week later Will was pacing back and forth with the piece of paper in his hand working up the nerve to call. He closed his office door so no one would disturb him and punched the number into his cell phone, pausing his finger over the 'call' button trying to queue up his nerve. *It's not a rocket destruct-sequence, Will. PUSH THE BUTTON.*

He heard her voice, now familiar, greet him at the other end of the phone.

"Samantha? It's Will Thompkins…from the hospital."

"Will, it's so good to hear from you. How are you?" *She hadn't forgotten him!*

"I'm fine, how are *you*?"

"Much better. I'm actually walking in a nearly upright position, as evolution intended." He smiled. There was a new energy in her voice.

"Great, you're healing then."

"Absolutely…can you hang on a second, Will, I just found a parking place, I'm putting the phone down." Will could hear the car shifting in the background. "Got it!"

"Samantha…you're not supposed to be driving, didn't Ira tell you?"

"He did, but this was kind of an emergency."

"What *kind* of emergency?"

"I am completely out of Peets tea. I didn't want to bother my friend Meg for it, because she lives across town, so I took a short drive."

"Tea is not an emergency, Professor Parrish."

"It is for *me*, Dr. Thompkins." As long as I can walk reasonably upright into Peets to get it, I wont be deterred."

"You haven't even got your stitches out yet…"

She laughed. "I think we better change the subject."

"I was calling to see if you'd like to go to dinner next week…only if you're feeling up to it."

"How about tonight, at my house. I'm bored out of my mind. I can cook something for you."

"That sounds great. But no cooking, why don't I bring dinner. What are you in the mood for?"

"Maybe some chicken? I'm just down the street from *Poulet*, I could pick one up…"

"*I'll* get it. Please drive yourself home immediately after getting your tea or Ira will accuse me of sabotaging his medical reputation."

"That's a deal." Can you come at six? It's not very cosmopolitan, I know, but I start to fade by nine."

"Six it is then."

"I look forward to it, Will."

"Me too, Samantha." He shut off the phone and realized he was grinning like a teenager.

He knocked at the door of the Craftsman bungalow on Walnut Street at six o'clock exactly. Samantha Parrish opened the door with a wide smile.

"You found it," she said, waving him in. He was struck by how animated and lovely she was. There was color in her face, and a lively mischievous quality in her eyes where the pain and exhaustion had been. She was dressed in a blue cotton dress the color of a robin's egg, and her hair was brushed straight down and tucked behind her ears. She wore small, translucent blue stone earrings that swayed whenever she gestured.

"I'm a fourth generation Berkeleyan, I can find anything in this town." He handed her a bouquet of flowers he picked out from a nearby street vendor. "These are for you."

She lit up. "Peonies, my favorite."

"I heard you gave all your flowers away to the other patients on the floor."

"It seemed like the right thing to do—I was escaping and they weren't." She grinned, and he found her so endearing he had to keep reeling himself back in.

"You know it's a little intimidating going out with you, I'm competing with a couple dozen 20-year olds, they're a lot more wily than me."

She laughed. "No, believe me, they're adorable, but *clueless*."

"These are for you, too." He held up two grocery bags full of food. Samantha peeked into them.

"Oh—wine, soup, veggies, and….Peet's tea…lots of it!"

"I thought maybe you'd stay put if I brought you provisions."

"How sweet of you, thank you." She kissed his cheek, and Will felt himself being pulled in again by the intoxicating scent of flowers. "It all looks delicious, follow me to the kitchen and I'll put it away."

"No, I can put it all away, you sit and direct me." He set down the bags and began emptying them, opening the worn oak cupboard doors, searching out where things went as she sat at the small kitchen table nearby. "This is a nice little house."

"Thanks, I just bought it last year. I'm so proud of it. It's expensive to live in Berkeley, a lot more expensive than Washington or Maine. Where do you live?

"Over by the Claremont Hotel."

"Oh, that's a beautiful part of town, what street?"

"…Avalon."

"*The* Avalon Street? In one of those grand old houses? Will was always a little surprised by how people reacted to the house on Avalon, to him it was just home.

"Actually, I inherited it from my parents. And they inherited it from my dad's parents, so it's been in the family a long time. How about some wine with the chicken?"

"Sounds delicious." He set out the plates of food and glasses of wine and sat down across from her at the table. It was nestled under a corner window in the tiny kitchen looking out onto the back porch, where freshly planted pots of ivy and fern jostled for space on a weathered wooden deck. Beyond, two large white camellia bushes in full bloom dominated the tiny yard. A late-afternoon light still streamed through the window, softly illuminating the kitchen as it faded into evening.

Their conversation flowed easily as always, and as the time passed they circled in to more intimate aspects of their lives.

"If you don't mind, Will, I'd love to hear more about your parents. They sound like they were extraordinary people."

"No, I don't mind. I like talking about them, actually. I try to remember everything I can." He took a big swallow of wine and let the memories wash over him. "My mother was from Florence. She came to Cal on a music scholarship when she was seventeen. She was a brilliant violinist, a prodigy, she'd been playing professionally since she was twelve. She was beautiful, luminous. All my friends were shamelessly infatuated with her. They would hang around playing basketball in the front yard hoping she'd call us in for something to eat, and then they'd sit around the kitchen table falling all over themselves trying to impress her. My father never got tired of telling the story of how they first met. He was cutting through the music building on his way to his American history lecture when he heard the sound of her violin coming from one of the practice rooms. She was playing Puccini, *Vissi D'Arte*, and he said the music was so intoxicating that as hard as he tried to keep on his path to the lecture he felt compelled to search out who was playing it. He said the moment he looked through the glass window of the practice room and saw her face, he knew he wanted to spend the rest of his life with her. By the time they were twenty they were married and she was pregnant with me. They were extraordinary people, passionate about everything—family, friends, books, music, food, art, politics, each other—especially each other. They were absolutely incorrigible about public displays of affection, you couldn't leave them alone in a room together without coming back to find them making out!" He smiled at the memory and then grew silent. "They were only forty-six when they died...a car accident." He was surprised to find himself choking on the words, the pain suddenly fresh, as if time and distance had contracted.

Samantha listened intently, remembering the pain of losing her own father. "It must have been devastating to lose them both so young with no warning. No wonder you have that pain in your eyes." Will winced, and veered his glance out the window onto the white camellias, now glowing in the evening light among their dark leaves. She saw the sadness flicker across his face and changed the subject. "What about your siblings, do they live near you?"

"My brother Dave lives in Marin. He's an orthopedic surgeon there, and he works here at Mercy a few days a week. Jules and Dan are both at Cal, they're twins."

"Did you all go to Berkeley?"

"Oh yeah, we're a Cal family—seasons tickets to all sporting events, blue and gold family room, trash-talking Stanford, the whole package." He laughed.

"I'm so envious! That's what I always imagined it would be like to have siblings."

"It's not always easy, especially with Dan and Jules—worrying about their school work, frat parties, drinking, driving, whether they're having safe sex...believe me, it's non-stop worry."

"They must be young...?"

"They just turned 18." He could see her doing the math in her head. He knew he was in deep now.

"How old were they when your parents...?"

"Four."

"Oh—you *raised* them." She tried to suppress the surprise in her voice.

"I did," he was relieved it was out in the open. "They're my children, at least that's how I've always thought of them. They needed to be someone's children, and I was it. After my parents died, I moved back into the house on Avalon and picked up the pieces. We've been the three musketeers ever since. We all still live together there, even Dave sometimes when he's in town." He leaned back in his chair and took a big gulp of wine and looked into her eyes to gauge her reaction. "Well that's kind of a relief. I usually save that information for the third date. You're good at this."

"Oh god, I'm sorry. I'm always trying to work out people's stories, it's a terrible habit. My friend Meg says it's the English major in me. That's probably why I don't *get* to the third date!"

"I never get *past* the third date." He laughed. "Once women hear my story they usually run the other direction!" She took in his face intently, as if she was seeing him for the first time.

"No one ever got to be interesting by having a seamless life." She said softly. "It must have so been hard—starting out as a young doctor, losing your parents and suddenly becoming the father of two small children. How did you do it?"

"It was overwhelming at first; we were all like walking wounded. But then, somehow we found our way. And it's been a *good* life, believe me, I wouldn't trade it for anything. Maria, our nanny, took care of them as if they were her own children after my mother was gone. And my friend Lee moved three doors down and helped me raise them—we went to so many recitals, soccer games and back-to-school nights people thought we were a gay couple. After awhile we didn't even bother correcting them."

Samantha laughed out loud. "That is a good friend."

"I *know*." He smiled at the memories of those early years. "So…I actually consider myself very lucky. I know that sounds crazy to some people, but as hard as it was at times we've made a great life together. My mother had a favorite saying, "Dove è il dono? *Where's the gift?*" She believed that no matter what disappointment or hardship came to you, there was always something to be gained by it. We used to make fun of her, because she had such Italian optimism about life. Then one weekend, when I was about 12, we were on a camping trip in Yosemite, one of my father's infamous treks into the wild. We'd been driving for hours, it was late, and my dad was trying to set up the tent in the dark to get my mother and Dave and I out of the cold. Just as we all got inside, it started to rain, and as it did, the tent collapsed on us. It was too dark and wet to fix it, so we used it as a tarp, with our bodies lined up underneath it to stay dry and our heads sticking out so we could breathe, rain rolling off our faces. My father was teasing my mother, asking her, "where's the gift now, Maria?" And then just as we laid our heads back on our rolled up jackets, the rain stopped and we looked up to see the night sky come alive with a meteor shower—hundreds of shooting stars, as if a cosmic magician was conjuring them out of his bag. I think that was the first time I finally got what she meant."

"And your children were the last gift from your parents…"

"Yes," Will said quietly. At that moment he realized he was in deeper than he had ever been with a woman. They finished eating their meal and sipped on the wine in a pleasant lull, each caught in their own thoughts.

"Do you have any pictures of them?"

"I have an *embarrassing* amount." He laughed and reached in his back pocket to find his wallet, pulling out an accordion of photos that burst open and dangled down several feet in front of him. "Since I've already shamelessly broken the first-date protocol, I might as well share these too," he laughed. She pored over them, taking in the details of the faces as he captioned them: "This is when they were five, just starting kindergarten, major separation anxiety—for *me* more than them; and here they were eight—off at camp, I was a nervous wreck when they were away. These are at the prom—those years almost killed me; and this is them now, they had it taken this year for father's day. My boy even shaved—a rarity."

"Oh, they're beautiful, Will. They look just like you—the family resemblance is so strong."

"I can't take any credit, it's all my parents doing." Will could see she was repositioning herself in the chair trying to stay comfortable. "Why don't we move to the living room where you can stretch out."

"Good idea. I just realized sitting in this chair is killing me." She walked tentatively to the couch and sat down, stretching her legs across the ottoman. "Much better." Will sat next to her, sinking into the down cushions. He looked around the room. The house was small, but charming, feminine. The walls were painted a pale, leafy green and the room was filled with furniture slipcovered in cream linen. Botanical prints, stacks of books and intimate family photographs were scattered about. In the bay window, bathed in early evening light, a lovely, worn terracotta bust of a young girl sat looking out from a rustic wooden table.

"That's a beautiful sculpture," he said, struck by the sweetness of the girl's expression. It reminded him of Jules.

"I bought it at an antique shop in Kensington. I just couldn't leave her. I must have gone in and out of that shop a dozen times trying to walk away, but she was *speaking* to me... in spite of what my bank account was trying to argue back!" She laughed and then turned pensive. "I think she reminds me of who I'm supposed to be." He looked closely at her curled up on the couch next to him, her blue eyes sentient.

"I can't imagine that you aren't already who you're supposed to be," he said.

"It's hard to know, isn't it? I read somewhere once, 'Life is filled with possibilities…and sometimes just the *memory* of possibilities.'" Will thought for a moment about his own life… how much of it had been only the memory of possibilities?

They talked until after ten o'clock. He didn't want to leave, but he could see fatigue overtaking her.

"I *have* to go. As much as I hate to end this conversation, you look exhausted. I'm sorry for keeping you up so late."

"No, the time went so fast, I haven't even noticed."

"Me too. Can't remember a better night." They looked at each other with anticipation until he couldn't resist another minute. He leaned over, held her chin in his hand and kissed her. The scent of her hair and the touch of her lips on him tinged with wine sent a charge through him that traveled straight to his groin. She leaned into his kiss, cupping both her hands around his face, gently sucking on his lower lip until he felt himself starting to lose control, his body hypersensitive to her touch.

"Will you come and visit again?" He answered by pressing his mouth to her lips. This time he pulled her body in close, feeling the softness of her breasts pressed against him underneath the blue cotton dress. The fragrance of her skin as she leaned in to kiss him overpowered him with desire. She was intoxicating. He came to his senses and pulled himself back. *She was still healing!* "I *really* should go."

"Okay," she let out a deep breath. "I'll walk you to the door."

"No, I can walk myself. You sit. I'll call you in a day or two and we'll see about a real dinner."

"That sounds good."

"Talk soon then...?"

"Soon. Bye Will."

"Bye Samantha."

"You can call me Sam, everyone else does."

"Okay then, bye *Sam*." He got to the door, but retreated to kiss her one more time, pressing into her and delicately stroking the soft nape of her neck. She kissed him hard, pulling him in closer.

"Okay, now I'm *really* going." He said, taking a deep breath.

"Me too—well, to bed, anyway. Alone—of course!" She giggled.

"Sleep tight...don't let the bedbugs bite."

"Okay, I wont." She grinned, and it seemed to Will that the whole room lit up. He shut the door and walked out into the damp night, still hot with her kiss.

By the time he got home, the inevitable panic set in. He picked up the phone to call Lee.

"Hey, how did the date go?"

"Amazing. She's kind and beautiful and so intuitive and ...I don't know, intoxicating."

"That's fantastic, good for you."

"No, it's NOT good, it's too much! I think I'm getting in too deep."

"Will, it's your first date. You can't possibly be in too deep, you hardly know her. You're just panicking because you're finally dating someone with the potential for a real relationship. Did you have sex?"

"Of *course* not! She hasn't even got her stitches out. Besides, she's not that kind of woman. She's *different*."

"Then what makes you think you're in too deep?"

"I don't know, she's so incredible. I feel like there's no way to go but deep."

"Okay, then why don't you just breathe into it and see where it goes. Maybe she's the one."

"I'm not ready for *the ONE!*' I have the kids and work… I'M NOT READY!" He was talking rapid-fire now; Lee could hear him launching into a full-on anxiety attack.

"Do you want me to come over?"

"No, it won't do any good. I know when I'm in too deep. I SHOWED HER PICTURES OF MY KIDS! I've got to get out of it!" The phone clicked off.

Will lay in bed staring at the ceiling trying to imagine how he would call Samantha to explain he couldn't see her again. She would think he was a total jerk, just like her cheating lawyer ex-boyfriend, but it was the only thing to do, he had to walk away before he got in any deeper. Why did he tell her about his parents? Why did he show her pictures of his kids—WHAT WAS HE THINKING? He didn't want to hurt her, but anything was better than the pain he was in now. He got up from the bed and walked down to the kitchen.

Everything reminded him of Samantha. Wine, Peets coffee, the leftover chicken in the fridge…*where did these robin's-egg blue napkins come from!* His heart was racing and his hands were getting numb. He was in full-throttle panic. He went back upstairs into the bathroom to find the valium Lee had prescribed for him last year when Dan and Jules flew to Europe with Eleanor. He fumbled in the medicine cabinet and found the bottle behind the shaving cream. He took two and laid down in bed waiting for them to take hold, trying to focus on his breathing by doing the exercise the hospital therapists taught for stress relief. Deep breath…exhale…deep breath…exhale… deep breath…he took his pulse: 140! He tried visualization, but all he could see was her expressive face—her eyes as blue as the sky, the soft nape of her neck… he checked his watch again…30 minutes. WHY WASN'T THE VALIUM WORKING? He felt like a cheetah in a National Geographic documentary, flailing as they shot it over and over with tranquilizer darts.

He stared at the ceiling, the ghosts of his past relationships swinging monkey-like through his mind. Marilyn Hartman— his first time…she was a goddess. They had sex in the carriage loft behind her parent's house when he was 17. He thought he was going to marry her. She went off to Yale and called him once, a pity call. Sashra Patel in medical school. She was brilliant and exotic, with her pierced nose and skin the color of latte—she went back to India and married a surgeon, breaking his heart. Katrina—gentle, free-spirited Katrina. How he ached back then for the silky folds of her body…where is she now? Bali? Amsterdam? Paris? And Miranda in her glass palace—that white fur rug, her teeth teasing him, her taut thighs…her soft breasts beneath her robin's-egg blue cotton dress…*wait…*

nineteen

Three days later he was standing on the front mat of Samantha Parrish's house on Walnut Street talking himself down. *It's just a date!* Lee was right, she didn't hold any magical power over him, he had overreacted. He wasn't going to let himself get so emotional this time, he had simply been overwhelmed by first-date euphoria. He repeated this mantra to himself several times as he knocked at the door, listening for her footsteps anxiously as she came to let him in.

The moment he saw her in the doorway all rationale was lost. She beamed as she greeted him, leaning up to kiss him on the cheek, the familiar scent of flowers wafting from her skin— *was it lavender?* Her hair was braided up loosely into a clip, with wisps of it falling down seductively on her neck and tucked behind her ears. "You look beautiful," he said, gazing at her face as he fell down the rabbit hole again.

"I'm so much better," she gushed, I got my stitches out!" Her blue eyes were full of life. She looked radiant in a white dress and silver sandals, a bracelet of silvery charms dangling from her wrist.

"Good for you," He smiled at her as he felt himself tumbling deeper.

He walked through the entryway into the soft green walls of the house. It already felt familiar to him. He started to sit on the couch next to her, but decided it was wiser if he sat in a nearby chair. She handed him a glass of wine and he took a big drink to steady himself. "So what did Ira say? Is everything okay?"

"Yes, all good, except for the bright red scar. There's now serious doubt I'm going to make the cover of 'Sports Illustrated'—a fine career thwarted."

He laughed. "What about your heart—did you see the cardiologist?"

"I'm working on it. And how about that worrying problem of yours, Dr. Thompkins? How is that going?"

"I'm working on it," he lied, his entire body flushed with free-floating anxiety even as the words came out of his mouth.

"Good, that's a start."

"Where would you like to go to dinner?"

"Well now that I have my mental acuity back, how about some place quiet where we can talk?"

"I've got just the place."

They climbed up the creaking wooden stairs to Chez Panisse, the enticing smell of spices from the kitchen greeting them at the entrance filling Will with nostalgia. The waitress seated them in his favorite booth and he ordered wine. Samantha sat across from him quietly, leaning her head back, breathing in the smell of fresh rosemary wafting from chicken roasting on the open grill. She took in the surroundings, fixing on the French cinema posters gracing the walls.

"Do you know this restaurant is one of the reasons I moved to Berkeley?"

"Really?" Will was always surprised when the things he took for granted had fame outside of his rarified little world.

She rested her elbows on the table and leaned forward to tell the story, her face tantalizingly close to his, the scent of her perfume wafting in the air between them.

"It's kind of a long story…"

"I have all the time in the world."

"Okay then, you've been warned," she teased. "When I was a little girl, my father used to take me to an old cinema outside of Boothbay where they played foreign movies. It was a long drive, in the winter it would sometimes take us more than an hour through the snow. When he was young he spent a year living in Paris hoping to become a painter before he came back to the States to settle down and enter medical school, and while he was there he fell in love with the films of a French writer named Marcel Pagnol—do you know him?" Will shook his head. He had no knowledge of French writers or French films, but he was so captivated listening to her telling the story he began to wish he'd paid more attention in his sophomore film class.

"Pagnol made a trilogy of movies called 'Marius,' 'Fanny,' and 'Cesar' about waterfront life in Marseille. They're tender films, full of colorful characters and all the little dramas of their lives. No matter how many times we saw those films, my father would sit captivated, watching the black and white scratchy images flickering across the screen, throwing his head back and laughing at his favorite parts. They were subtitled, so I couldn't always read the dialogue fast enough, but he would lean in close and whisper explanations of things I didn't understand. I loved the conspiracy, the two of us watching together in the dark the-ater—sometimes we were the only ones in the seats, you know Maine wasn't exactly a mecca for French cinema, and I would watch my father's eyes brighten as the vignettes lit across the screen—the waterfront shops and the fishmongers and the narrow streets of Marseille, the way everyone kept their nose in everyone's business, but also the affection they had for each other, the decency underlying it all. His favorite character was Honoré Panisse, an older man who falls in love with a young woman named Fanny who is unmarried and pregnant. He's a gentle-hearted soul, and he offers to marry Fanny in order to save her honor. Whenever I slipped up in life, my dad would recite his favorite line from from Honore Panisse: 'Sam,' he would say, 'One cannot live without doing wrong.'" She smiled at the memory and pointed to one of the black and white cin-ema portraits hanging on the restaurant wall. "That's Panisse's photograph over there. And that one is his Fanny…Alice named her daughter after her."

Will gazed at her across the table as she spoke, her blue eyes lit up with memories. He imagined her as the nascent ver-sion of her present self, sitting next to her father in the theater, the black and white film dancing across their faces. He thought he never wanted to leave the booth, that he could stay with her there in that restaurant, the restaurant that his parents loved, the restaurant he had loved since he was a child—and listen to her tell stories for days.

"My parents were friends with Alice," he said at last, "from the old days when she was first starting this restaurant. They used to bring us here all the time when I was young, we celebrated practically every birthday and anniversary here—even me getting into medical school. I've been bringing Danny and Jules here since they were little—Alice watched them grow up—we all watched Fanny grow up. You know, in all the years we've been coming here, I never realized that's where the name Chez Panisse came from."

Samantha laughed and leaned back into the booth, putting the glass of wine to her lips. "You should dine with English majors more often."

He looked around the restaurant and the memories flowed back to him. He saw his mother laughing, her head thrown back, curls bouncing, his father with a wide smile, his arm resting on her leg, his fingers spread across her knee, unable to sit through even a single dinner without the comfort of her body entwined in his. He thought of how many meals they had shared together, the fragrant dishes of food spread across the table. How they would sample off each others plates, dipping crusted sourdough bread into olive oil, and then, at the end of the meal, into thick hot chocolate that steamed up into their faces.

"How old were you when your father died?" He asked at last, breaking his reverie.

"Thirteen. Sometimes it feels as painful as if it just happened. It's cruel the way traumatic events engrave themselves into your memory. As though they're carved in ivory—the years wash over them, blurring the edges, but the cut is never quite erased. The thing I remember most was coming back to the house after the funeral— the *silence*. My mother staring at his things, his plaid flannel robe hanging from its hook on the door, his books and his shoes strewn casually, his favorite coffee mug sitting on the kitchen counter as if he was going to come back to drink from it. We didn't really know how to go on, you know? Like someone had cut a gaping hole in the curtain of our little universe, and we were suddenly seeing through to the darkness on the other side. Our hearts felt scalded, hardened so that they couldn't ever expand again to the size they had once been. The only thing that gave me any relief was burying myself in books. I went to the library and checked out as many as I could and kept them stacked by my bed and in my backpack. I took them to the dinner table and the schoolyard. In the summer I would go to the harbor to sit on the warm wood of the old pier and read. I would spend hours watching the fishermen load and unload their boats, letting myself be mesmerized by the silvery fish jumping around in their nets in the sun. I wanted to travel any place where I could escape the ache of his absence."

They were silent for a moment. The memory of his own parents caused the old ache to ripple through Will's chest along its familiar path.

Samantha tried to break the melancholy. "Have you ever been to Paris?"

"Many times. When I was young my parents took Dave and me there—and to Italy, during sabbaticals or if my mother had a concert. But I'm ashamed to say I hardly remember any of it. I was so busy secretly scolding them for wasting so much time strolling through shops and museums and sidewalk cafes. My mother would usually have rehearsals in the morning, so Dave and I would tag along with my father. He would spend half a day poking around the ragged antique bookstores of the Latin Quarter, bargaining with shopkeepers for rare books and old prints and manuscripts. Later we'd meet up with her, and the two of them would pore over his purchases, lingering for hours over coffee or wine in their favorite bistros, ordering round after round of small plates of food, eating and making idle conversation with waiters and other diners and passersby. I was so impatient with them, I must have been insufferable to travel with. I stupidly thought we should all be home getting back to work on our 'real life.' Little did I know, that *was* real life. I'd give anything now to have those days back with them."

"How about you, do you like Paris?"

She grinned. "Paris is *always* a good idea."

They lingered over their food at a leisurely pace, embroidering on the stories of their lives. He shared his fears about raising his children, trying to keep his parents' memories alive for them, the strains and heartaches of his job. She told him her fear about whether she could make a life in Berkeley so far from the world where she had grown up, her pain of finding out about the infidelity of her ex, her loneliness and embarrassment. With every turn of the conversation, Will fell more deeply, crazily under her spell.

By the time they reached her house their conversation had turned to intimate whispers and they were all over each other. She nestled next to him on the couch, her breasts soft and warm against his chest, her arms and legs draped over him. He wanted her so badly, his erection pressed against her.

"Only one more week to wait," she said, her breath hot in his ear.

"I'm pretty sure Ira said two." He corrected her, trying to reign himself in.

She pressed tighter against him and cupped his face in her hands. "Two is too long." She said, kissing his lower lip and gently circling it with her tongue. "What Ira doesn't know won't hurt him."

"So that's what my patients say when I'm not around." Will teased, "Nice to know, Ms. P." With her scent and the warmth of her full breasts next to him, he was starting to lose control. He lifted her off gently and collected himself, kissing her one last time. "I've just had the image of Ira wagging his finger at me, it's definitely time for me to go."

They said their goodbyes at the door reluctantly. "See you next week?"

"Yes, next week."

"I'll call before then."

"Okay."

"Possibly in the next five minutes from the car."

"That would be perfectly acceptable."

"I'm off then."

She put her fingers to his lips as they stood in the doorway, and his body heated up with her touch. When she closed the door Will felt as if the world suddenly went dark.

Four days later, Lee's phone was ringing.

"Hey, what are you doing?"

"I'm *sleeping*. What time is it?"

"It's only 12:30, old man."

"I have no reason to stay awake, my love life sucks. Let me guess, you can't sleep because of Samantha."

"I haven't slept in four nights. I've got 'Kill Bill,' want to watch it…?" Silence.

"…It's *Uma*."

"All right, come over, I'll make some coffee."

Will walked through the door looking wide-eyed and disheveled.

"Geeze, you look like hell. Why don't you take something to help you sleep?"

"I'm trying to go cold turkey to prove to-myself I can do it."

"It's not working."

"No shit."

"I really can't see 'Kill Bill' as a sleep aid."

"I've given up sleeping, I'm just trying to take my mind off things 'till I can see her again."

"So am I expected to give up sleeping too?"

Will ignored him and slid the disc in to launch the movie. "Why aren't you dating?"

"I don't know, I've lost interest in the pursuit, I'm getting too old." Lee leaned back into the couch and took a sip of coffee. "To tell you the truth I'm rethinking my casual dating philosophy. I'm looking for someone I can have a meaningful relationship with. That's a way shallower pool of women than I'm used to operating in. It's not easy being discriminating."

"Wow, this is new for you."

"Yeah, I don't know what's wrong with me, it took me way too long to grow up. I was still dating Brazilian models when I should've been looking for someone serious. I'm a little past the package date now."

"Don't be ridiculous, you're a charming guy…in your own way."

"I'm thinking of asking Karen Winslow out again."

"The psychologist?"

"Yeah."

"She's fantastic, I *always* liked her."

"Yeah, I really blew it with her. My head wasn't in the right place. But we've been talking lately, you know she works in the hospital a few days a week, and I feel like there's still something there. I want to take it slow, because she might decide she doesn't want to go down that road again with me, you know? I was kind of an asshole. I'm trying to show her I'm a different guy."

"You know she was my therapist a few years back when I was going through that stuff with Eleanor and the kids?"

"Yeah, I know."

"So I could never socialize with you guys, she knows what a neurotic basket case I am."

"It's not like there's any news there."

"What if I need her again? Do I have to give her up as a therapist? Because my mental health is more important than your need to settle down."

"I don't think there's any rule about my girlfriend being your therapist, but thanks for the selfless loyalty. By the way, if I needed any evidence that I have to make a change in my life, watching "Kill Bill" with you at 1:00 a.m. is it."

"Wait…shut up, I *love* this part…" Will said, as Uma launched into another slow-motion bloody battle with her arch-nemesis, Lucy Liu.

twenty

Will was sitting in a restaurant booth across from Samantha listening to her tell a story, when he realized he was in deeper than he had ever been with a woman. He was so blissfully happy in her company, he ignored the waves of panic that occasionally rippled through his chest making it hard to breathe. He was now in a full-blown relationship. They had been together numerous times, and every time it was easier, better. He thought about her constantly—the sound of her voice, her laugh, her soft breasts and the curve of her back when he held her; he was intoxicated with her. He was lost in that thought when he was jolted out of his reverie by the buzz of his phone. He cringed when he saw the number appear. *Jules*. He still hadn't told either of the kids about Samantha; he wasn't ready for those two worlds to collide. He briefly thought about not answering the phone, but even though they were in college, he was still too tethered to ignore a call. The attachment was ingrained in his nervous system, as if an invisible neural cord ran through the three of them—if any part of it tugged, his entire central nervous system responded.

"Sorry, it's Jules, she's at Lake Tahoe with friends…It'll just take a second," he apologized. He clicked on the phone.

"What's up?" He tried to keep it short before Jules figured out he was with a date. She could read him like a bar code.

"Are you busy?"

"I'm actually in a restaurant. Everything okay up there?"

"Yeah, the weather is great, we're headed for the lake in a minute. Are you with a *date*?"

Here we go. "Why?"

"Oh my god, you *are* with a date! How exciting, where did you meet her?"

"At the hospital."

"A doctor?"

"No, thankfully not a doctor—not that kind anyway."

"What's she like?"

"She's smart and beautiful and very patient to let me talk on the phone to you while she's sitting across from me."

"Oh, sorry…take a pic of her with your cell and text it to me."

"Juliana!"

"Okay, okay, go back to your meal, I'll grill you later."

He winced. "Be careful on the lake…"

"*Goodbye.*"

"Bye." He turned to Samantha. "Sorry, it's the worry thing, hard to break the habit. I'm all yours now."

"Don't be silly, it's touching that you're all so close, they obviously still rely on you."

"Yeah, they're 18 but not quite ready to be cut loose. Jules feels the need to manage my love life. Not that it's a big job, by the way."

"I'll bet."

"No, believe me, raising two teenagers and doing my job 12-14 hours a day, there hasn't been a whole lot of time for romance. My love life has pretty much been DNR for the last few years."

"DNR? *Oh*, Do Not Resuscitate." She laughed. "It must be a little easier now that they're in college."

"Yeah, they're pretty independent now. Now that I'm exhausted from raising them and completely unmarketable, they've got lives of their own."

"Will Thompkins, you are far from being unmarketable."

"I don't know about that Ms. P., your instincts were compromised when you met me."

"Come here," she pulled his chin toward her and began to kiss him. "My instincts are impeccable," she whispered in a low voice into his ear. She punctuated it by running her lips from his earlobe down his neck, sending an electric current directly to his groin. "And do you know what tonight is?" Will was too overcome with lust to remember his own name. "Tonight is our eighth date. It's more than 4 weeks since that fateful morning I swept you off your feet by throwing up on you." She moved her lips to his mouth as she ran her finger slowly up his thigh. "And that means it's one day after Ira gave me the green light."

He returned her kiss hotly, squeezing her thigh under the table. "What are you suggesting?"

"That you might want to skip dessert tonight."

"I'd be happy to, except since you put your hand on my thigh I can't get up from this table without embarrassing myself."

"I can wait."

"Would you like to come to my house?" he said, ignoring the current of anxiety shooting into his chest. "Everyone is gone for the weekend, we could have it to ourselves." He felt slightly disembodied as the words came out of his mouth, as if he was on the outside watching himself speak.

"Really? The *whole* house? Including your bedroom?"

"Especially my bedroom." He took a deep breath, "Want to spend the night?" Another shot of adrenalin.

"A sleepover?"

"Well, I don't know how much sleeping will be involved, but there is a bed."

"*Yes.*"

Samantha stood in the entryway of the house on Avalon and took it all in—the hand-carved redwood beams that stretched high overhead, the tall paned windows, their beveled glass looking out onto the tree-lined street, the winding staircase with its curved oak bannister, the warm wood paneling lined with oil paintings and the well-worn leather furniture arranged on colorful Persian rugs. "It's beautiful Will. I've passed the outside of this house dozens of times on my walks...I always wondered about the people who lived here."

"Well now you know," he said, squeezing her around the waist. "A neurotic doctor, two teenagers and a dog. I hope it's not too much of a letdown." He thought about offering to show her around the house, but when she took her coat off the sight of her in the black dress, her long earrings dangling tantalizingly onto the nape of her neck, made him too crazy with lust to play tour guide. He couldn't think of anything but getting her into his bed and making love to her.

The truth was he had never had sex with a woman in his bedroom. It lay fallow since his parents vacated it so suddenly all those years ago. Until now, he could never bring himself to violate the grace of their love, the passion that had given rise to four children.

He took her hand and pulled her up the stairs. They stood at the foot of his bed as he held her at arms length for a moment, illuminated by the street lamps outside the bedroom window. The light glowed across her face, along the wisps of her hair and the soft curves of her body. He kissed her forehead and traced his way down her nose to her lips, nibbling on them gently, then down the graceful curve of her neck. He slid off the straps of her dress to kiss her bare shoulders, and her knees began to melt as he unzipped it, sliding it down to her hips. He kissed the soft white inside of her arm, tracing a line to her tender wrist, where he could feel her pulse racing. He put his lips to her breasts cupping them softly in his hands, pressing his mouth around them. Her knees gave into him as she let him hold her up with his arms while she pressed herself against him, her eyes closed, her head thrown back, engulfed in his touch.

He lifted her up and she wrapped her legs around him, her arms circling his neck, as he laid her down on his bed. He finished sliding off her dress, kissing the soft inside of her thighs, running his lips and tongue across the soft flesh of her stomach. He shed his clothes and laid next to her, wild with lust, pressed up against her.

"Come inside me…" she ran her hand tantalizingly along the length of him.

"Are you sure? I don't want to hurt you…"

"I'm sure, don't worry."

"Okay, promise you'll tell me…if it's too soon."

"I promise."

He held her gently. Her breath was hot in his ear. She ran her soft lips down his neck and he was lost, succumbed to her, feeling himself deep inside, lost in the fertile secrets of her body, her breasts full and pressed against his chest, her soft thighs open to him. She laid her head back on the pillow and closed her eyes. He pressed his mouth onto her neck taking in her fragrance as he moved into her, her hips rising to meet him. They continued in a hypnotic rhythm, their breath now pulsing in sync with their bodies, rising and falling, their skin growing hotter with each thrust, as if an electric current was running between them, until neither of them could bear to hold off any longer and they exploded in relief, collapsing into the pillows. They laid there, spent, the evening light from the bedroom window drifting over their naked bodies, the quiet broken only by the sound of their breathing.

"You are intoxicating." He said when he finally could gather his thoughts to speak. She smiled, her hair spread out across his pillow, her face flush with heat.

"So are you."

He kissed her breasts and lay next to her, stroking her body, tenderly tracing his fingers around the bright red scar that brought her to him.

She turned over and wrapped one leg and arm over him, resting her head on the pillow so she could look into his eyes, and gently touched her lips to each eyelid. "I wish I could take the worry out of those eyes."

He raised himself up on his arm and looked at her intently. "I'm not worried now, not when I'm with you. When I'm with you the rest of the world goes away. You're like a little galaxy of your own—Samantha world. No clanging gurneys, no blood, no pain, no worry…just your skin and the smell of lavender." He cupped her face in his hand and kissed her mouth again. Then he took in her face. "You look tired."

"I suddenly feel *exhausted*," she said, dropping back down on the pillow.

"You're still healing. Why don't you curl up here next to me and go to sleep.

She curled up under his arm with her leg draped over him, her breasts pressed against him and fell asleep. He could feel her heart beating against him. It was rapid and pounding. Did he hear an arrhythmia? "Sam, he whispered," did you ever see the cardiologist?" But she was already too deep in sleep to hear him. He put his fingers to her wrist and rested it on him, feeling her pulse against his chest, watching her for as long as he could until he drifted off himself, into the kind of deep slumber that had eluded him since the day he met her.

In the morning, when the sun filtered through the thick glass of the old wood-paned windows into the bedroom, Will felt disoriented to find Samantha Parrish sleeping peacefully beside him. How many years had it been since he'd woken up with anyone next to him in his bed? Only one of his children, feverish or frightened by a bad dream. He felt a twinge of melancholy at the thought of so many years spent alone… "the memory of possibility." Outside the bedroom window, from the corner of his line of vision, he saw a hummingbird hovering in mid air, the sun reflecting off its crimson head as it fed on the bougainvillea flowers that bloomed along the east side of the house. In spite of the frantic beating of its wings, it appeared to be frozen in time, hanging motionless in mid air. He held it in his sight as long as he could, not wanting to break the illusion that life was holding still. He looked over at Samantha, curled up, breathing softly on the pillow. When he turned back to the window, the hummingbird was gone. He quietly slipped out of bed and went down the stairs to the kitchen. By the time he brought tea up to her she was sitting up, arranging her hair with her fingers, her bare feet dangling off the edge of the bed.

"That t-shirt never looked so good." He smiled at her.

"I guess I should pack for alternate scenarios when I go to dinner with you." She grinned back at him.

"I like this scenario just fine." He kissed the curve of her neck where she had pulled back her hair. The smell of perfume and sex on her skin made him feel intoxicated again. "I made you some tea."

"Very sweet. Perfect sleepover etiquette. You must have a lot of practice."

"No, the only regular sleepover date in this room is the dog. He has very modest culinary needs—although he does snore. And drool."

She laughed and took the cup from him. "This bedroom is beautiful," she said, looking around as the sun filled the room reflecting off the mustard-colored walls and warm cherry furniture. "Did you decorate it yourself?"

"Yes, if that includes pointing to a page in the Pottery Barn catalogue and having Dave and Jules go out and get it for me. I *did* write the check. But then with two college kids I write the check for everything."

"Well you chose admirably. It's lovely."

"I was going to take you on a tour of the house last night, but that black dress intervened."

"How about now?"

"Now is perfect. As long as you walk behind me so I'm not tempted by seeing you in that t-shirt."

"That's a deal." She slipped off the bed and put her arms around him from behind, nuzzling his neck. "How's this?"

"That isn't much help." He could already feel himself getting aroused. "Better walk beside me." He took her hand and pulled her next to him. "What do you want to see first?"

"These pictures," she pulled him across the room to a wall filled with large family photos. They were framed in thick wood, in varying sizes, and hung in rows from floor to ceiling where they could be seen easily across from the bed. "They look like they're full of stories," she said, her eyes scanning the faces, looking out at her as if they'd been freshly captured. "Will you tell me about them?"

"Sure, where should I start?"

"How about this one." She pointed to a photo of two skinny, freckled boys dangling a fish from a line, grinning.

"That's Dave and me on one of my father's infamous camping trips, somewhere off the John Muir trail. He used to spend hours poring over wilderness maps trying to find new places to explore; I can't tell you how many times we wound up lost at the edge of a cliff or in the middle of a mosquito-infested marsh with him scratching his head looking at his map. It drove my mother crazy."

"And is this Maria?"

He nodded and gazed fondly on the photo of Maria in a bright turquoise dress splashed with yellow sunflowers, her ample arms stretched around Danny and Jules. "She was forever showing up at the breakfast table in a new dress. She sewed them herself, and she always made a miniature copy for Jules. They would run around Berkeley in their matching outfits—all the neighborhood shopkeepers knew them.

"How about this one...Lee?"

"Yeah, that's him letting the kids put the sold sign on his house down the street. They were so excited he was moving in."

"They were so small..."

"Yeah, he's been with us since the beginning. He moved in with us the day after my parents died and pretty much never left."

"This one is adorable." She pointed to a photo of Will with Danny and Jules. Both children were dressed in plaid and navy blue, their hands deep in his pockets, eyes wide, wearing reticent smiles.

"First day of kindergarten. Lee took it. They hung on me like that for a good year after my parents were gone, Maria had to keep sewing my pockets back up. Lee called us the six-legged-monster." He pointed to another photo. "That's him and me in medical school. Look at those haircuts, we thought we were so cool." They both laughed. "And this," he pointed to a photo of a boy caught in mid air, spread-eagled, squealing with delight, "is Danny jumping off the high-dive. He was only six—fearless! I was a nervous wreck."

"And this must be your parents." She pointed to the large black-and-white photo in the center of all the others. A young couple, their eyes wide and full of life, arms wrapped around each other, were smiling into the camera.

"That's them." They were beautiful, weren't they? So crazy about each other. Crazy about life. A passionate life, but a short one." Samantha clenched his hand.

"This wall is amazing Will…all these stories…it's your whole world."

"I know." He grew pensive for a moment. "Whenever I think about how I've screwed up my life, I come here and it makes me feel better."

She turned to him and looked hard into his eyes. "Will Thompkins, you have *not* screwed up your life. You've raised two beautiful children and taken care of a thousand sick people. You are a *good man*."

The words pierced him. "I'm a man with a lot of baggage," he said softly. They continued ambling through the old house, finally making their way downstairs to the big sunny kitchen for breakfast, where they sat at the old redwood table eating their scrambled eggs and bacon, talking easily. To Will it seemed there was never enough time to finish the conversation, it always led easily from one topic to the next, as if they had a whole lifetime of stories and memories to catch up on. When they finally finished it was almost noon, and the threat of everyone pouring back into the house sent them both upstairs to dress. She gathered her things, leaving the t-shirt folded neatly on the bed. They stood near the bedroom window across from the wall of framed photos and kissed one last time. Outside, the crimson-headed hummingbird hovered at the bougainvillea and then zipped away.

twenty-one

"So, our boy seems to be dating pretty seriously now," Mike said, setting up the folding table for poker, "You must be happy."

Lee grabbed a beer from the fridge. "The jury is still out on that."

"Why...you don't like her?"

"No, I think she's terrific, it's just that he has a habit of self-immolating."

"I don't know, I've never seen him this smitten before."

"Yeah, that's what worries me, she actually makes him happy."

Their conversation was interrupted by Seth and Will arriving. They grabbed beers from the fridge and settled into their usual places at the table. Mike wasted no time testing the waters.

"So, seems like things are getting pretty serious with the professor." Will flinched. "You dating exclusively now?"

"Yeah, pretty much." Will shuffled the cards and started to deal, hoping to distract his interrogator, but Mike wasn't having it.

"Think she might be the one?"

Lee looked up from his cards to see Will's reaction. Will squirmed in his chair.

"We're just dating."

Lee rolled his eyes.

"What was that for?" Will said testily.

"What?"

"You rolled your eyes."

"I'm just saying..."

"Saying what?" Will slapped the remainder of the deck down in the middle of the table.

"It just occurs to me that you're possibly uncomfortable with the idea of finding 'the one.'"

"Can we move on to another topic?"

"Case in point."

"Ladies, don't get your panties in a twist, I'm sorry I brought up the subject. I just happened to see her in Seth's office the other day and I was curious how things were going. It's no big deal." Will's antennae went up.

"She was in your office? Is she your patient?"

Seth looked trapped. "She's...a patient."

"Are you treating her for the arrhythmia?"

Seth was annoyed. "I know you're not asking me for a patient's confidential information…"

"She's not just a patient, she's my girlfriend."

"Oh, excuse me, that's different then. Let me just email you her entire medical history, I mean after all, she's your 'girlfriend.'"

"I thought you said it wasn't serious." Mike chimed in.

"It's not." Will was trapped, but he wasn't letting go. "Are you medicating her for it?"

"I'm not having this discussion, Will."

"I'm the one who found the arrhythmia, you know."

"I'm not discussing this."

"Because if she's in any kind of danger it seems like I should know."

"Are you going to bet or do you pass?" Seth was not budging.

"I mean, what if something happened on a date, it would be helpful to know."

"What would you be doing on a date to cause 'something' to happen?" Mike goaded.

"Drop it Will." Seth was resolute.

Will went silent. The conversation shifted to football and the prospects of Cal's draft picks for the new season, but when he walked the short distance back home that night, Will was still brooding.

twenty-two

"So, out with Samantha again last night," Dave probed his older brother as they sat at the kitchen table drinking coffee.

"How many months does that make?"

"I don't know." Will lied.

"four, five...?"

"That sounds about right."

"Wow, that's good for you—you must really like her."

Will was silent.

"Why don't you bring her here to meet us?"

Will tried to kill the subject. "I'll think about it."

"What's to think about? Invite her over for dinner. I'd like to meet her, and the kids are always nagging you about your personal life." Dave had been living at the house more frequently in the years since his divorce, spending more time with Dan and Jules, often staying the night in his old studio upstairs on the weekends. He liked to prepare elaborate meals, gathering them all around the big redwood table to eat together the way they did before college and social activities scattered them to the wind.

"Maybe in a couple of weeks."

"Why wait, how about this Saturday?"

Will cringed. He dreaded bringing his personal life into the world on Avalon; it confused everything. Avalon was the world he shared with his children. It was where he grew up as a boy, the world of his parents. It was too messy mixing it up with a woman, especially with a woman he was falling so hard for. Nothing good could come of the two worlds colliding. "I don't know, Dave…"

"It's just dinner, Will. Take the leap. I'll make that Cajun pork roast you like. Ask her."

"We don't even know if the kids can be here…"

"I'll make them be here. Ask her."

Will was cornered. "Okay, I'll see if she's free."

"I'd love to come!" Samantha was enthusiastic.

"Are you sure? They're probably going to grill you relentlessly."

"I'll grill them right back."

"That can't be good for *me*."

"What time?"

"Around seven, I can pick you up."

"Don't be silly, I'll drive over."

Will spent the day anxiously, secretly hoping something would happen that would cause the dinner to be cancelled. Samantha knocked at the door at 7:00 exactly, greeting him with an absent kiss.

"Is my hair sticking out? I'm so nervous."

"It's perfect. Don't be nervous," he said, mostly to himself. "Come on, they're in the kitchen, they're all dying to meet you."

The three of them were waiting for Samantha around the old redwood table, the fragrance of the roast and spices filling the big kitchen. They were noisy and cheerful and inquisitive. Jules, especially, was excited to have another woman in the house.

Maria had retired to Margarita's farm. After fifteen years of keeping her sacred vow to her beloved Maria Gambiari, it was time for her to leave the house on Avalon. With Dan and Jules off to college and Will working long hours, she spent most of her days alone, watching her favorite Spanish soaps, sewing and cooking elaborate evening meals in the hope they would bring the whole family around the table together as in the old days. But as often as not only one or two of them would show up, and the leftover food would be spooned into plastic containers and stored in the refrigerator to be eaten later. When at last she came to Will to tell him she thought she could be more useful at the farm helping Margarita, he reluctantly agreed, although the thought of walking into the house without her there was almost unbearable to him.

But it was Jules who missed her the most. Surrounded by three brothers for most of her life, she had lost her only feminine ally in the house, her kindred spirit. Sometimes, on a weekend when she didn't have a concert, she would drive out to Margarita's farm and they would go to the farmers market together as they did in the old days, coming home to make homemade tortillas, forming the thick balls of dough with their hands, spreading them out onto the white flour with the rolling pin as they sang to music blaring from the Spanish radio station. At night, when the rest of the farm was asleep, they would curl up in bed talking softly, analyzing the idiosyncrasies of various family members, comparing them to characters in Maria's soaps until they drifted peacefully off to sleep, the smell of fertile soil and the sounds of crickets and farm animals carried in the breeze through the open bedroom window.

Jules was thrilled her older brother was finally dating seriously. It seemed to her all he did was work and worry over her and her brothers. For as long as she could remember he seemed to carry a pain and weariness in his eyes that nothing could extinguish.

"So how did you meet?" She queried Samantha. "Will won't tell us."

"He won't?"

Will squirmed in his chair. "Here we go…"

"It was very romantic, I threw up on him!"

"*What*?" They all started laughing.

"Yeah, I had appendicitis and my friend Ann brought me into emergency. Your brother came in to examine me, and just as he was getting ready to leave, I threw up. And the worst part is I was in so much pain I didn't care. I vaguely remember thinking, 'he's very handsome, I wish I hadn't thrown up on him,' but he didn't seem to mind."

"Nah, I get thrown up on all the time—by my patients and my kids. Although not usually my dates."

"So *that's* the story," Dave said. "You asked her out when she had appendicitis?"

"Of course not. I waited until Ira did an appendectomy and I asked her out when she was discharged. It was all very ethical. Although I did think she was the most beautiful appy patient I ever had."

"Yeah, I'm sure I was really attractive doubled over in pain throwing up. Okay, that's enough about me, how about you two? Will has bragged so much about you…"

"Oh god, he's so embarrassing, did he take out that roll of pictures he has of us?"

"He did!"

"*Will!*"

"I spent 15 years raising you, I should be able to brag a little. Or have you forgotten… Vacuuming the dog? Tossing my car keys down the laundry chute and sending Jules down to retrieve them with my date in the living room…we could hear her screaming through the vent the whole way down. Or how about Danny trying to fly off of Maria's roof with homemade glider wings. Your pediatrician had to vouch for me so they didn't call Child Protective Services. Not to mention the teenage years, they almost killed me. Where do you think I got this grey hair?" He ran his hand across his peppered hair to make the point.

"We've been hearing about how we gave him grey hair for years." Jules countered. "Everyone who knows him knows he was *born* worrying. We were the only kids at school who had personal earthquake emergency kits in our backpacks—including goggles and a solar radio! He used to have Maria pack our lunches with the apples and carrots pre-cut into little bits 'So you don't choke.'"

"How about the fire drills?" Dan chimed in. "He would put on a red Stanford sweatshirt with a sign taped across his chest that said, 'FIRE!' Then he'd set off the house alarm and make us find a safe exit while he randomly jumped in front of us waving his arms yelling, 'NO EXIT—FIRE IS ALREADY HERE! FIND ANOTHER WAY OUT!'"

"One time Danny was so tired he just laid in the middle of the hallway and said, 'I'm dead, save Jules.'"

"I still get freaked out when I see a Stanford sweatshirt."

Will winced, "Okay, okay, I was a slightly neurotic parent…"

"How about going to Hawaii on spring break and finding a pack of condoms tucked in my suitcase with a note that said, 'No questions asked, but USE YOUR HEAD!'"

"Oh, and that gross skin cancer brochure that popped out of my make-up bag when I was putting on lip-gloss—I was mortified!"

"Nice impression you're making on my date, thank you for the support. Can we *please* talk about something else?" Will pleaded.

"Jules has a concert at Stanford next month," Dan offered, glancing sideways at Will. "You should come. You can meet our grandmother." Will felt his stomach tighten—his two worlds were melding way too quickly.

"I can get you a free ticket." Jules said, "It would be so much fun. We all go to Chez Panisse first—it's on Will."

"What do you mean, 'It's on Will?' *Everything* is on me."

"I would love to come. You're all so accomplished. When I was your age I was earning my way through college working at the Boothbay Sears candy counter selling popcorn."

"Listen, when we were at Cal, Will and I bagged groceries at Andronico's—it was my dad's idea of building character. Since we both wanted to be doctors he said it would help us to work with our hands and deal with people."

"Juliana, how did you ever survive with all these brothers?"

"Oh my god, don't get me started."

"Please don't." Will winced.

"What did we do for entertainment? —Season tickets to *all* Cal games. What kind of movies did we see? —Bruce Willis or Samuel L. Jackson. What did we do on weekends? —Played basketball and watched sports on television. And try taking them shopping for a dress. You would think I was taking them into a foreign country—a third-world country they couldn't wait to get out of. And god forbid you want to have a good cry. They just stand there with their hands in their pockets looking shell-shocked, like a foreign object dropped into the middle of the room. Absolutely clueless…"

They finished dinner in a flurry of conversation, never leaving the kitchen or the old wooden table. "You know, I actually set the dining room up intending to serve a proper din-ner," Dave apologized.

"This is such a great kitchen. I can't imagine why you'd ever want to eat anywhere else," Samantha said, surveying the soft yellow walls and natural pine woodwork. "This table is beautiful," she ran her hands along the worn redwood.

Jules rolled her eyes, "Please don't get Will started on the history of the table, we'll never get out of here."

"Maybe we should make her do 'What did you learn today?'" Dan teased.

"I think you've tortured her enough for the night." Will intervened. "How about we go into the living room and get away from this food before I eat another bite."

Dave began clearing the table as the others settled in the living room, the food and wine creating a pleasant lull.

Samantha broke the quiet at last. "Juliana, I would love to hear you play…would you mind playing something for us?"

"Of course!" She bounded up the stairs and returned with the violin just as Dave joined them in the living room.

"What would you like to hear?" She said, eager to please.

"Whatever you'd like to play."

Jules thought for a moment. "How about the theme from *Cinema Paradiso*, it's one of my favorites. We always get more tips when I play it—feel free!" she pointed to the open violin case, grinning.

She drew the bow across the strings of the Stradivarius and the rich, warm sound began to fill the room. The melody was poignant, sweet and sad, and she teased out the notes tenderly, sending them circling into the air to hover around them, casting her spell. As always, she played from memory, closing her eyes, her body leaning in to the phrasing of the music—grazioso, legato, con dolente. The four of them fell quiet, sitting rapt as she caressed the strings sensitively, pulling exquisite sounds from the heart of the instrument, the aged wood resonating its honeyed tone. Suddenly, as the notes enveloped him, Will felt an unexpected ripple of pain rise into his throat. He saw his mother playing for them all in the same room, animated and joyful, his father leaning back in his leather chair watching her in rapturous content. He felt overwhelmed by a deep longing for his boyhood, before time and death tore everything apart. All at once, the memories and heartache cast a dark shadow over him.

When Jules finished playing the room went silent, as if they were waiting for the notes to float back to earth.

"Juliana that was…breathtaking." Samantha said, breaking the silence. Her eyes were welling with tears, and she looked away from Will so he couldn't see her. "I've never heard that piece played more poignantly, so lovely and sad."

"It is sad, isn't it." Jules replied. "I always try to imagine what he was thinking of when he wrote it. It's so beautiful, and yet it seems to be full of loss."

"Yes…that's it—beautifully sad. Mono no aware." Samantha said softly.

Will turned to her. "What was that phrase you used?' He tried to look into her eyes, but they were still cast downward blinking back tears.

"Mono no aware…it means beautiful sadness…"

"My father used to describe my mother's playing that way. I never heard anyone use that expression besides him."

She looked up and their eyes met briefly, but now it was Will turning away to avoid her.

"Whose ready for dessert?" Dave carried out plates of cherry cobbler and the conversation turned to food and small talk. But as the evening wound down, Will could not shake his melancholy. Samantha saw that he had grown pensive and silent. Finally, after a round of hugs and goodbyes, it was time for her to leave. Will walked her out into the damp evening air to her car.

"Thank you for inviting me." She said quietly. "You were right, you *are* lucky. They're wonderful Will, they're your shooting stars."

He kissed her goodnight and held her for a long while, breathing in the fragrance of her and feeling the soft warmth of her body against the evening cold. He helped her get into the car to drive away to her house on Walnut Street, to its leaf green walls and the terra cotta bust of the girl bathed in moonlight that held the mystery of who she was, "the memory of possibilities." He waved goodbye, and as he watched the car disappear into the darkness, his heart ached knowing that he would leave her.

twenty-three

They were lying in Samantha's bed when his phone buzzed with an early morning text.

Will stared at the screen. "Sorry Sam, I have to go in."

"But…what about our picnic…I have everything packed." She sat up in bed.

"I know, I'm sorry, they're shorthanded, can we try for another day?" He leaned over and kissed her, but she didn't respond. He got out of bed and began to pull his clothes on. She was quiet.

"Don't look so sad. I'll check with you later, maybe we can grab dinner."

"Mmm hmm."

"Samantha, my work is…"

"I know, Will, it's not the work."

"What is it then?"

"It's that you work more now than you did when we were first together. It seems like the closer we get, the more your work pulls you away. I'm starting to think it's *me* you're running away from."

"Sam…no. I'm not running away from you…"

"Are you sure? Because I'd rather you tell me now instead of making excuses. I'm in this pretty deep, Will. I'd rather know now before I go any deeper."

"Sam, you're the best thing that ever happened to me, I'm not running away from you, I promise. It's just work, that's all."

"There isn't…anyone else, is there?" Her voice was plaintive, tinged with the old wound. The words stung Will. He couldn't believe she would think that of him. He leaned over the bed and held her face with both his hands, looking into her eyes.

"No. *No.* There's *never* been anyone else, not since the day I met you. I'm not like Richard. Understand?" He kissed her, feeling her body stiffen as he did. He finished dressing and grabbed his keys. He looked back at her one last time sitting at the edge of the bed, her shoulders slumped in defeat. Even though he saw the pain in her eyes, he couldn't stop himself from leaving.

When he came home from the hospital and walked into the kitchen, Dave was putting away the last of dinner. The smell of Italian spices lingering in the kitchen filled Will with melancholy.

"Hey, how was your picnic with Sam?"

"I didn't make it, I got called into work." He shuffled uneasily and leaned against the counter.

"Really? That's the third weekend in a row. You're working an awful lot for a guy who's in charge."

"Well, I told them I was available."

"When you had a day planned with Samantha? Why?"

"We were shorthanded."

Dave stopped what he was doing and turned to face him. "Is everything okay between you two?"

"Yeah, why?"

"I don't know, seems like you might be trying to avoid spending time with her."

"Things are fine."

Dave eyed him suspiciously. "Are you worried you're getting too close?" He stared hard into his older brother's eyes. "Take my advice, someone like Sam doesn't come along every day. Don't lose her. You'll be sorry if you do."

"I know."

"Do you?"

Will rose up on his feet, ready to bolt. "Where are the kids?"

"Dan's out and Jules is playing at Adagia."

"How long is she there?"

"I think she's playing until 11:00."

"Okay, I'm going to go catch her."

"You want some company?"

"No." The abruptness of his reply startled even Will. "Sorry...I'm just not very good company right now."

"Okay. You want something to eat before you go? I made lasagna."

"No, thanks, I'm not hungry."

Will drove the mile or so to Adagia, the little restaurant across from campus where Juliana's quartet was playing. He needed to free his mind from the events of that day. It was a habit he had since the kids were little. Whenever he felt overwhelmed by life in the ER, he would slip away to see them—sometimes he would surprise them and pick them up from school. They would squeal with delight when they saw him, squirming like puppies and throwing their arms around him pressing their little faces up against his cheek. Sometimes he would just stand at the edge of the schoolyard at lunchtime and watch them play, hanging from the monkey bars, trading baseball cards, laughing with their friends. The sight of them healthy and happy was like a balm to him.

As soon as he walked through the door of the restaurant he could hear the sweet strains of Juliana's violin. The quartet sat on the small raised wooden stage at the rear of the café, and when she saw him come in she smiled at him. He ordered a scotch and stood watching her from the bar. She was not his scrawny little girl anymore. Her face was sculpted and expressive, her curls, which Maria had always struggled to contain, were now held back elegantly from her face with a black velvet tie. She was slender, but her body, wrapped gracefully in a black dress, was the body of a woman. When did it happen? He could still remember the little girl who would curl up on his lap like a cat, nestling her head on his chest, afraid to leave him.

He took a sip of scotch and listened to her play, waiting for the alcohol to dull his pain. She was playing Paganini. He couldn't remember the particular piece it was, most of the melodies he knew by instinct, from listening as a boy. His mother would try to teach him the proper names of the classical pieces, but he couldn't make them stick. He only knew that when she played them her dark brown eyes would light up and the soft curls around her face would bounce as she moved her body in sync with her bow, and the whole house, his whole world, would feel happy and safe. "Mio amore!" She would greet him whenever he ran for her embrace, wrapping her arms around him, pressing his cheek up to her soft skin and the delicious fragrance of her body. "Il mio bambino," She would purr as she covered him with kisses. Now the music coming from the stage began to make his chest feel tight. Was it his heart aching? *God, he missed her.*

"She sure can play, can't she?" Will's reverie was broken by the bartender addressing him.

"Yes she can." Will took another drink of scotch.

"I'm a hip-hop and blues guy myself, but her playing is so beautiful she can melt the ice in your glass." Will studied him closer. He was a lanky, good looking African-American kid with an easy smile.

"Do you get to hear her play often?" Will probed.

"Often as I can. I only work here a few nights a week, I'm at Boalt."

"Ah. Law school, that's a hard road."

"Tell me about it."

"You're a doctor."

"How did you know?"

"My dad's a doctor, went to school at UCSF."

"Me too…is it that obvious?"

The bartender reached over and tugged at Will's stethoscope poking out from under his jacket collar. "Well, this was a dead-giveaway." He smiled and handed the scope to Will.

"Oh," Will laughed, tucking the stethoscope into his jacket pocket. "An absent-minded doctor."

"I'm Jason." The bartender put out his hand.

"Nice to meet you Jason, I'm Will." He said, shaking it. "Does your dad still practice here?"

"No, Chicago. That's where I'm originally from. He has a family practice and my mom's a schoolteacher there."

"Doing the lord's own work then." Will said.

"That they are," the bartender smiled.

The quartet finished playing and took a break. Juliana came over to join Will in the bar.

"Beautiful fiddling as always Jules," the bartender said. Will could see he was under her spell.

"Thanks Jason," She smiled coyly back at him.

"I didn't know you were coming," she kissed Will, guiding him away from the bar over to a table. "Did you have to work late? Where's Sam?"

"I did work late and Sam is home, busy with schoolwork too." He lied. "Do you want something to eat?" He tried to veer away from the subject.

"Some tea would be nice." He called over the waitress.

"You should eat something, Jules…"

"I'm fine," she put two fingers up to the lines in his forehead, "Stop worrying."

The server came to take their order.

"I'll have a Chai tea…"

"And another Glenlivit." Will chimed in.

The server returned in a few minutes with their drinks. "I just want to tell you, your playing is so beautiful. Whenever you play we get bigger tips." the young woman gushed. "Drinks are on the house."

"Oh thanks. Nice to know I'm good for business!" Jules laughed.

"I especially love the La Boheme pieces, my favorite."

"Me too. I'll play one next for you, maybe you'll get more tips—always like to support my fellow workers." Will smiled. She was Henry Thompkins' girl, equalitarian to the bone.

"So tell me how you're doing with Samantha, Will. I love her *so* much, she fits in our family. I feel like she's the one for you. Do you love her?"

Will panicked. "Jules…"

"Come on Will, you've been dating for almost six months, *do* you…?"

"I care about her a *lot*."

"Oh, *God*. Is that what you say to her? You 'care a lot?'"

"Juliana, it's complicated…"

"No, it's not Will, it's *not*. You tell us you love us a dozen times a day. It's not that hard. I think you do love her, but you're afraid to tell her, you're afraid to make the commitment. Have you even told her how much she means to you?"

"Not exactly."

"Oh god. Give me some of that." She poured the scotch from his glass into her tea.

"Since when do you drink scotch?" He protested.

"Since you became so clueless about your love life." She took a gulp.

He tried again to deflect the line of interrogation. "I'm not clueless, okay, I appreciate that Samantha is an incredible woman."

"Then you better tell her, Will. You better let her know or you'll lose her. Do you hear me?"

"I hear you."

Jules saw the cellist signaling her from across the room. "Okay, time's up, I've got to go make some money for these people." She drained the last of the fortified tea. "Mmmm. I needed that," she grinned and kissed him on the cheek, heading back to the stage. She raised the violin to her shoulder and began to play *Vissi D'Arte*, the crowd growing quiet as the sad melody filled the room. Will swallowed the last of the Glenlivit and headed out of the restaurant before more pain set in.

He drove home looking for some relief. Dave's car was gone, probably headed back to Marin. Thank god. He knew his brother meant well, but he wasn't in the mood to continue that conversation. The house was dark and quiet, except for Max, the dog, who greeted him enthusiastically, oblivious to his pain. He was too restless to sleep, so he went upstairs and wandered down the hall to see if Dan was home yet, but there was no sign of him. He stood inside the walls of the familiar bedroom, which had been his own room when he was a child, and his father's before that. He stared down at the old wooden floor, dented and worn from all the years of rambunctious boys traversing it, and then out the window, where he could see the oak tree rustling in the breeze, calling him outside. When he was a boy he would climb through the window onto the roof, shimmying down the tree's great boughs to the thrill of whatever adventure awaited at the bottom. Now he felt disoriented—who was standing there—the boy or the man? The room was piled with clothes and sports equipment and an indecipherable twist of video editing paraphernalia—multiple laptops wired in a maze of cords to various sized screens and speakers and power modules. Gone were the dinosaurs and legos and Power Ranger sheets. He walked over to the bookshelf where a much-worn stuffed Big Bird still held his own against the tide of adulthood, his matted fur a testament to years of adoration. He picked it up and held it in his hands, its google eyes staring back at him in a perpetual expression of childhood wonder. He held it up to his face trying to breathe in the scent of his little boy, but it only smelled of dust and fake fur. Max shuffled at Will's feet, looking up at him, unsure why they were lingering. 'The boy isn't here,' he seemed to be saying to Will.

Will felt the tears welling up in his eyes. He sat on the bed and let them flow…for his children who he knew he could not hold close for much longer, for his parents who left him too soon, and for himself, who he knew could not be saved.

twenty-four

"So how are things working out with Samantha?" Lee queried, aiming straight into the crosshairs.

"Fine." Will lied, taking a bite of his sandwich to avoid the discussion.

"Really? Because I'm sensing some backsliding."

"There's no backsliding."

"You worked three weekends in a row."

"We were understaffed."

You're the Chief of Emergency Medicine, you couldn't get an attending to step in?

"Look, I'm just taking it slow, that's all. It's not a big deal."

"Or maybe you're getting too close and you're having commitment issues?"

Here we go.

"Maybe you think you don't deserve to be happy."

"That's ridiculous."

"Maybe you have some crazy notion that being happy with Samantha is somehow 'tempting fate'?"

"Can we change the subject?"

"No."

Will felt physical pain talking about Samantha. "Please…?"

Lee relented, sensing his friend was in trouble. "I'm trying to help, Will. I think it would be a huge mistake to lose her, I just don't want you to fuck it up."

Will was silent.

"Did you pick up the tickets for the Goldman Ball?"

"Not yet."

"Are you going?"

"Yes."

"Are you taking Sam?"

"Of course."

"You have to be there, you know. For the award…"

Will made a face. "You know how I feel about that…"

"Well the Goldman people feel otherwise. You have to be there…there'll be hell to pay if you're not."

Will stood up from the table to leave, his food still on the plate.

Lee locked in on him. "I'm trying to save you from yourself, buddy."

"I know. I just...I don't think I can be saved." He turned away from his friend and walked out of the cafeteria down to the ER. Down to the world of blood and hurt and wounded souls waiting to be rescued, the only world that made sense to him now.

"Hey it's me, Karen and I are heading to the Claremont around 6:00, want us to pick you and Sam up?"

"Are you worried I wont show?"

"Slightly, yes, but mostly I just thought it would be convenient."

"To deliver me personally, so you could be sure?"

"Don't be an asshole Will."

"I'm going to pick up Samantha and take her there myself."

"Great. That sounds fine, I'll see you there around 6:30 then."

"Okay."

"Did you finish your speech?"

"Yes, mom, I finished it."

"Okay, see you later then."

"Bye."

The Goldman Foundation Ball was the social event of the year for doctors. It was held at the Claremont Hotel ballroom and was the hospital's version of the senior prom. This year Will had been voted the equivalent of prom king, a dubious honor as far as he was concerned. He didn't believe in awards, he had a file drawer full of them and they meant no more to him than the obligatory trophies handed out to kids on soccer teams every season. If everyone did their job, there would be no need for awards, being a good doctor would just be the norm.

Henry Thompkins had a quote that hung over his old wooden desk, written by hand on worn note paper, given to him by his own father. "Study hard, think quietly, act frankly, talk gently." To that Henry Thompkins had added two things, in his own hand, "Acknowledge the contributions of others," "Don't be fooled by praise." Will had lived by those words his entire life, just as his father had. He'd learned the hard way never to be taken in by praise. In the ER, life was so capricious, one minute you could be lauded for saving a life and the next you were standing in front of a shell-shocked relative telling them their brother, or mother, or child was lost. It wasn't wise to get cocky, it was all but guaranteed fate would slap you back to the mat an instant later.

Cocktails began at 6:00. He planned to go to Samantha's house at 5:30, bring her flowers and share a glass of champagne privately before they went. He wanted to prove to her that he was able to make a commitment to their relationship, even though he was almost incapacitated by anxiety about whether he could actually do it.

Everyone was calling to check on him, Dave offered to help him with his tux, Jules wanted to pick out Samantha's flowers, Danny wanted to record him giving his speech in case he needed to fine tune it, Lee wanted to personally deliver him to the hotel. He felt pathetic.

At 4:30 he realized he had forgotten to email his speech to himself. It was on his computer desktop at the hospital. It was no big deal, he could be there in 10 minutes, print it out, and still be at Sam's by 5:30. He put on the tux and headed to Mercy, flowers and champagne in the front seat. The Goldman event would be a chance to introduce Samantha to people, to show her he was serious about their relationship. He was starting to feel better.

He got to the hospital and went straight to his office, avoiding walking through the ER, as he usually did, so he wouldn't get sucked in. He was at his desk printing the speech when his cell phone went off…

Lee was sitting with Karen at a banquet table nervously watching the door. It was 6:45 and Will wasn't there yet. At 7:00 he saw Dave come in and latched onto him.

"Have you seen Will?"

"No, he said he was heading over at 6:00 after he picked up Sam."

"It's a ten-minute drive from her house, they should be here by now. I called Jules, she says he left home hours ago. He's not answering his phone."

"Shit. What time do they announce the award?"

"8:00."

"Okay, there's still plenty of time, maybe they just got hung up, let's not panic."

"He's not exactly been a rock of stability lately, you know."

"I know, but he'd never *not* show up to this…*would he*?"

"We have to call Samantha. What if something happened to him? We have to call her to see if he's been in touch."

"Okay, let me call her, but let's wait another 10 minutes."

"He's gotten held up at the hospital." Samantha said. She sounded exasperated. He said he'd be here at 7:30."

"Anything we can do, do you want me to come get you?" Dave's worry turned to fury at Will's thoughtlessness.

"No thanks, I'll just wait for him."

"Okay, I'm sure he'll be there soon. Hang in there." Dave clicked off the phone and looked at Lee. "He went to the hospital."

"What…Why?"

"She didn't say, he said he'd pick her up at 7:30. You better tell the Goldman people he might be late."

Samantha stood in the living room fully decked out in a satin gown and jewelry she borrowed from Meg, trying to decide what to do. Dinner was at 8:00. If they got there by 7:45 they could still recover the evening. She would have a glass of wine as soon as they got there, and they could visit with everyone and get seated in time to avoid looking like they were too late. It would be okay. She was nervous and trying hard not to be angry. She wanted to sit down, but Meg's dress was so tight it would wrinkle, so she leaned against the counter standing straight up. She kicked off her heels and checked her hair in the mirror one more time. It looked good, not sticking out. Meg was a genius with hair. She paced back and forth waiting with her phone in her hand, checking the time. 7:45. Was he standing her up? No, he wouldn't do that. He'd been a little distant lately, but he was a good man, something must have happened. They must have needed him, he wouldn't leave her waiting on such an important night unless it was really urgent. 7:55. Now they were really late. Maybe no one would notice, maybe it would be crowded and noisy and they could slip in. She went to the refrigerator and poured a glass of wine. She hadn't eaten since noon and she was starving; she thought by now she would be eating hors d'oeuvres. She grabbed some cheese and crackers to absorb the wine, trying to eat the morsels carefully so her lipstick wouldn't smudge. Her stomach tightened with every excruciating minute that passed.

8:15. *Damn you, Will Thompkins…*

Lee stared at his phone and looked up at Dave. "You better tell the Goldman people he wont be here. He just emailed me his speech, he wants you to give it."

"Son of a bitch."

Will paced outside the operating room waiting for Ira Feinberg to give him word. He felt bad asking Ira to stay after a full day of surgery, but he trusted him more than anyone. He was sure they would have to remove the spleen, there was too much internal bleeding, but he hoped the kidneys hadn't been damaged. At least the CAT scan was negative, no subdural bleed, no scull fractures, thank God. He looked at his watch. 8:15. What was taking Ira so long? It had been over three hours, things must not be going well. The Goldman people… there was nothing he could do, they would just have to deal, he couldn't leave until he knew how the surgery went, he'd explain to them later. Dave could handle the speech, he was good at that sort of thing, and anyway god knows Will had saved his ass enough times. His chest felt tight and he was nauseous. He should call Samantha again…why isn't she picking up? 8:30. *Shit.* Everything was turning to shit.

It was nine o'clock when Will knocked at the door on Walnut Street. He had texted Sam that he was on his way, but she didn't reply and she wasn't picking up his calls. He knocked again and after an excruciating few minutes she opened the door. She looked stunning, dressed in a lavender satin ball gown that made her eyes look like deep pools of blue water.

"Sorry..."

"Uh huh." She kept the door only partially open, making it clear he was not coming in and she was not coming out.

"I got held up with a patient. I got away as soon as I could..."

He could see she was blinking back tears. He felt his chest tighten.

"We could still go...they're probably still serving dinner, there's dancing until midnight..."

"No, thanks, I...kind of have a headache, I think I'll call it a night."

"So sorry Sam, sorry. You look beautiful..."

She looked at him, at his tuxedo and the bouquet of flowers he was holding. "You too." She said. Then she shut the door.

Will put his palm up against the door, as if he would be able to feel her through it, but she had already stepped away. He could see her shadow in the living room through the sheer curtains. She was bent over and she was crying.

He didn't want to face anyone, so he went back to the hospital hoping to catch Ira, but he had already gone home. He put on a spare set of clothes from his office, relieved to get out of the tux and everything it reminded him of, and walked the halls. 11:30, she would be waking up soon. He went up to her room. She looked so fragile lying there, her arm and leg fractured, her face cut and bruised. Her blond hair was still caked with blood from the crash, brushed neatly into a ponytail by one of the nurses. The only thing recognizable was the perfect red manicure at the end of her slender fingers that had somehow managed to survive the mayhem. The thought of her using it to emphasize a point, or to seduce him with some playful sleight of hand made him smile. Fierce Miranda; she looked so vulnerable now. He sat in a chair next to her bed and watched her lying there, soundless except for the beep of the cardiac monitor. He used to think they were so different from each other, but now he wondered. Neither of them could manage to relinquish themselves to a relationship.

Wasn't there someone who loved her enough to come and comfort her? Was that why she asked the paramedics to call him? Why hadn't anyone come to see her? Only her law partners calling in to arrange for her to be moved to a private hospital in the city as soon as she was ready. He saw her stir and held her hand gently, kissing her red manicured fingers. She opened her eyes slowly and smiled when she saw him.

"Hey there." He said softly.

"Hey." She was groggy, trying to focus.

"How are you feeling?

"Better, seeing you."

"You gave me quite a scare."

"Sorry...idiot driver was texting."

"So I heard. It could be one hell of a lawsuit dealing with the likes of you...if you weren't that idiot driver."

"Non compos mentis." She smiled.

"Did Dr. Feinberg come and talk to you yet?"

"I can't remember…"

"He's the one who did the surgery on you. He's the best."

"Oh…he took something out…" She struggled to remember in the fog of the drugs.

"Your spleen. And one kidney. They were pretty badly damaged, there was a lot of bleeding. But the other kidney is fine, it'll do all the work now."

"Oh…" Her mouth quivered and she started to cry. He reached his arms around her to hug her gently, trying not to jostle her to cause any pain.

"It's okay, it's good to cry, let it out." She sobbed into his chest for a few minutes, and Will rocked her to soothe her, cradling her head. He laid her back down as she began to drift off.

"I made a mistake about you…" She grasped his hand. "Shouldn't have let you go." Before Will could answer, she fell back asleep.

The monitor beeped gently to the rhythms of her heart. He thought about their first meeting, how steely and self-assured, even formidable she seemed. He'd underestimated her then, hadn't foreseen her capacity for tenderness and loyalty. She'd saved his family when he was unable to save them himself, charging in, stilettos clacking, like a crimson knight ending Heather's siege. Will was forever in debt to her.

He smiled as he remembered her recounting the victory, tossing her head back laughing, ponytail swaying, martini in hand. She had vanquished the pre-nup in a brilliant twist of legal precedent and blackmail, the judge voiding it as "fraudu-lently induced," siding with Miranda's invocation of a landmark New York Appeals Court decision. The ruling was aided by the loquacious deposition of Heather's suddenly resurfaced ex-lov-er—a man with his own axe to grind.

Will let his thoughts drift as he watched the curves on the cardiac monitor rise and fall, the only other sound in the room the soft sound of Miranda breathing. He spent the night in the chair next to her bed, unable to bear the thought of her waking up alone and scared.

In the morning Ira deemed her stable enough for the short ride to the city, and a private ambulance came for her. Will kissed her goodbye and promised to visit as he watched them close the door and take her away to her world of glass and steel.

He showed up at Lee's door later that morning.

"Jesus, you look like something the dog dragged in. Where have you been?"

"The hospital."

"You have got a lot of people pissed off at you, cowboy."

"I know."

"You want to tell me what happened?"

"Not really."

"Have you called home? They're pretty worried."

"I left Dave a message to let him know I'm okay. I did intend to go, you know. I just…something happened."

"Okay."

"Did the speech go all right?"

"Yeah, it was a very good speech. It would've been better if you actually gave it yourself, but Dave did a good job. You're going to have to do some fence-mending with the Goldman people."

"I know. I'll think of something. Write a big check, I guess."

"What about Samantha?"

"I really screwed that up. She's not taking my calls."

"Can you blame her?"

"No."

"Are you relieved?"

"*No*. Jesus, I'm scared I've lost her."

"Well that's a start."

"A start for what? A life of loneliness and misery? I can't believe I fucked up so badly with her. She's possibly the only woman in the world who gets me."

"*Possibly…?*"

"What am I going to do?" He looked desperate.

"I don't know, try to talk to her…"

"I can't. I can't hurt her again." He felt his chest tighten remembering the sight of her crying through the window. He thought about Miranda, lying there hurt and bleeding on the gurney. "I've got to go."

"Why don't you come in, let's talk about this…"

"There's nothing to talk about. Everything I touch turns to shit. I'm going home to my kids."

twenty-five

The week following the Goldman Ball was a blur of misery for Will. Dan and Jules looked at him as though he
dropped in from another planet, Dave lectured him
every chance he got, and he had to deal with the ire of the hospital Chief and the Development team for the award fiasco.
The Goldman people, as he suspected, were placated by a large
donation on his behalf, but news of his no-show spread virally
through the hospital gossip circuits and soon his entire staff was
tiptoeing around him as if he was about to melt down at any
moment. Only Carlotta knew the whole story.

"How is the attorney doing?"

"A little better. I went to see her yesterday. She's out of ICU
they might release her next week. I put her in touch with that
nephrologist I know from UCSF, he's really good."

"How about Samantha?"

"She's not talking to me."

"I wouldn't either."

"Thanks, that really helps."

"You cannot leave a woman in a ball gown waiting for three and half hours. There will be hell to pay."

"Yeah, I got that memo."

"Have you tried sending her flowers?"

"Of course, I sent roses *and* a gift basket of Peet's tea."

"Mmm hmm." Well a gift basket of tea when you've been stood up in a ball gown is not much comfort."

"Will you stop saying 'ball gown' that way? It's not like I left her at the alter."

"Not exactly."

"She hasn't broken up with me yet. Do you think she's trying to hurt me?"

"No, I think she's trying to decide if she can get over this. You haven't exactly been the perfect boyfriend you know. She's 35. Women who are 35 are not going to waste time on a man who's not willing to make a commitment."

"Jesus, if one more person says the 'C' word to me I'm going to slash my wrists."

"Think about it."

"All I do is think about it, Carlotta. I can't sleep at night, I can't eat. I just *think.*"

She looked in his eyes and saw how much pain he was in and put her arms around him. "Listen, you and I have been through a lot of hard times together, a lot worse than this. You're going to figure it out, so don't give up on yourself. You can still be saved. The Lord does not give us more than we can handle."

"I don't know, Carlotta. Whoever's up there has seriously overestimated my capacity for pain."

twenty-six

"So Will, it's been awhile since we've seen each other."

Will sat across from Karen Winslow on a couch in her office, three floors above his own. He wasn't sure he wanted to be there. "Yeah, I've been doing pretty well, you know...until now."

"How are the kids?"

"Oh, they're great. Lee probably told you. They're just perfect, they're...my best work."

"So what brings you here?"

"Well, besides intense lobbying from my entire family?" He laughed nervously. "I seem to be losing control over the whole anxiety thing again." He crossed and uncrossed his legs trying to get comfortable. "I'm really screwing things up with the people I care about, and I can't seem to stop myself, I'm not sure why."

"Do you think there's something in particular that triggered it?"

"Well, a lot of things, mostly…Samantha." He fidgeted on the couch. "I don't know if you heard. She broke up with me." When he said it out loud he felt his chest ache.

"Oh, I didn't know. I'm sorry."

"Yeah, it happened a week ago. The whole Goldman ball thing, you know. She said she was afraid I wasn't committed to the relationship, and she was getting in too deep…I was hurting her."

"*Were* you committed to the relationship?"

"*Yes*. At least I felt like I was. I don't know…it's complicated. I've never been with a woman like her. I haven't been able to get her out of my mind since the day I met her. I don't know why that scares me so much, because she's amazing, you know, so sensitive and kind, and she gets me. The kids love her, *everyone* loves her. Jules warned me I was going to lose her, she said I should tell her I love her, but for some reason I just couldn't, and now she's gone." He winced as he said it. "Wow. It's hard to say that out loud. It's hard to believe she's not in my life any more…" The words caught in his throat. The pain in his chest became more intense, radiating out to his groin. *Jesus, what could possibly cause this much pain, was he having a heart attack? He ticked through the symptoms—nausea, chest pain, shortness of breath, fatigue…*

"*Do* you love her?"

"I don't know. I never really felt like this about a woman. When I'm with her I feel saner, happier. There's something about her—the soothing sound of her voice at night when we're in bed talking, the way she wraps her arms around me from behind and whispers to me, the beautiful curve of her back when she's lying next to me...when I was with her the whole rest of the world went away. Sometimes when she left the room I felt like the air had gone out of it." He felt another stab of pain pulse through him as he heard his words slip into past tense. "She... *redeemed* me."

Karen was silent for a moment as the words hung in the air.

"Why do you need redemption, Will...when did you fall from grace?"

He stood up. His heart was pounding in his ears, he couldn't get enough air in his lungs.

"I have to go..."

"Why do you think you need redemption," she persisted.

Now the pain was radiating from his chest through his whole body. His hands and feet felt numb. He looked down at her and choked out the words. "You *know*..." He was at the door now, swaying back and forth on his feet like a prizefighter waiting for the next punch. "I have to go..."

Karen could see he was in full-blown panic. "Please don't leave, Will. We don't have to talk if you don't want to. Let's do some breathing exercises together before you go. Please stay..."

He was hyperventilating. He focused on her face, trying to use her to pull himself back from the panic. Her eyes were familiar, compassionate. He felt the panic ease a little and walked back into the room, sitting tentatively on the edge of the couch in front of her. She began to talk calmly and steadily to him as they worked through the relaxation exercises, her voice soft, hypnotic, working like a salve on his wounds, until eventually he felt the tightness in his chest ease, his breathing return to normal. He had no concept of how much time had passed. When she signaled they were done, he felt an exhaustion so crushing that he could hardly raise himself up to leave.

"Would you like to come again next week?"

"Yes." He felt the tears welling up in his eyes. He headed for the hall, but then stopped himself in the doorway and turned back to look at her. "The thing is…I can't lose anyone else I love." His voice was plaintive.

"I know." She said, softly. And then he was gone, disappeared down the stairs.

He was too exhausted to drive home or talk to anyone, so he collapsed on the couch in his office and hit the button on his ipod. Amos Lee's 'Arms of a Woman' was playing on repeat.

As he walked from his car into the house, he could hear the intermittent roar of the Cal football game pulsing in the night from the stadium nearby. Dan and Jules would be at the game with their friends; he would have the house to himself. The sound of football was soothing to him, part of the familiar rhythm of growing up in the shadow of the University. The academic calendar, punctuated by football season, had paced all of their lives for as long as he could remember.

He was aching to go straight to bed, but as soon as he turned the key, Max greeted him excitedly, looking for a walk. Will was too exhausted to find the leash and take him around the block, so he shuffled out with him through the kitchen door into the back yard to give him some fresh air. As he did, the motion light on Maria's cottage came to life, illuminating its bright blue front door as if to suggest that someone was home. But the little house was empty and silent now, the bustle of activity that always seemed to surround it was gone.

It was his mother who had painted the door blue, to remind her of the colorful doors in the Italian countryside. How many times had he made the trip back and forth from the main house to that blue door—to drop off the kids when he had to work the night shift, or retrieve them when Maria needed a little peace, or sometimes just to visit her himself when he needed company after a long day in the ER. He fished for the key on his key ring and went inside. It was all there as Maria had left it, but now only the skeleton remained. There was the little sleeper sofa that she would open for Dan and Jules to curl up on during late nights, and the tiny kitchen, once filled with the smell of home-made tortillas, now cold and dark. Gone were all the personal treasures that had made it such a refuge—the family photos, the random toys, the baskets of thread and ribbon and her sewing machine that hummed along daily, concocting some new fashion out of the piles of colorful fabric she kept neatly stacked on a shelf nearby. The dog sniffed at the old smells in the cottage, hunting out past memories. A single bright pink ribbon poked out from beneath the couch, missed by Maria's eagle eye. Will picked it up and held it, feeling the silky smoothness between his fingers. He lingered for a moment, then put the ribbon in his pocket, turned off the lights and went back through the kitchen door into the house, Max following dutifully behind.

He headed up the stairs to bed, but his melancholy tugged at him, so he clicked open the door into the study and turned on the light, illuminating the rarified world that had been his father's retreat. The walls were lined with books, beautiful and worn, history books, books of maps, rare first editions, tattered old Penguin classics, modern novels and paperbacks—all mingled together in equalitarian glory to satisfy Henry Thompkins's voracious intellectual curiosity. Will walked over and sat in his father's old wooden chair and surveyed the glorious cacophony on the desk—letters, newspapers, handwritten notes and scholarly journals, a small bronze sculpture of the Greek god Hermes, pictures of his children and his wife mingled with old Thompkins family photos, all of it left exactly as it had been 15 years ago, Maria tenderly dusting around the piles as if Henry Thompkins would be coming home to take charge of the chaos again. Will's eyes rested on an old photo of himself—he looked about 14 years old—in full hiking gear, standing near a trail-head post, grinning. He picked it up to examine it. The trail sign said, "John Muir Trail," but he couldn't remember ever taking such a photo. He looked closer into the face, frozen in boyish enthusiasm, and saw that it was not him, but his father—or was it his grandfather? He turned on the desk lamp to examine it more closely, the eyes and the nose, the exuberant smile, but he couldn't discern for sure who it was, it was as though he had tumbled into a conundrum of time. He ran his fingers along the curves of the boy's image under the glass and then placed his palm over it as if to feel…what? His flesh? His spirit? Something intangible that he was trying to reach. He felt the pain in his chest again. He reached in his pocket and pulled out the pink ribbon and laid it gently on the desk among the other artifacts of his father's life. Then he went to bed, the dog trailing behind him.

twenty-seven

He was drinking his morning coffee in the kitchen when Dan shot the first arrow.

"Hey, can you drop me off at school on your way to the hospital?"

Will flinched. He hated going anywhere near the university where there was a chance of seeing Samantha. She loved walking the campus, she used any excuse to traverse its tree-lined footpaths and perimeters lined with busy coffee shops and cafes full of students. When they were together, Will would often pick her up on his way home from the hospital, pulling the car up to the curb to wait for her to materialize from between the buildings with her sack of books across her shoulders. He would always get a thrill when he saw her waving at him, her face lit up, smiling.

"Dan...can you get your sister to take you, I'm running a little late."

"She's not here, she spent the night at Jason's..." As soon as the words came out of his mouth Dan blanched, realizing what he had unleashed. He desperately tried to reel it back in. "Uh... what happened is that the game went late, so Jules took Jason home, because he needed a ride, and then a girlfriend of Jules, who just happens to live in the same house as Jason, offered to let her stay in *her* room because by then it was almost 2 a.m...." Will stared him down, boring through him.

"Save it."

Dan slumped in his chair.

"How long has this been going on?"

"What?" He tried again to feign ignorance.

"Them sleeping together."

Dan flailed like a moth on a hot lamp. "Well it's not like...I mean they've been dating for more than three months, you know."

Will rested his elbows on the old redwood table and dropped his head into his hands, rubbing his eyes, trying to wipe out the memories of the last few months and his household's steep descent.

"No, I didn't know." *He was a commando parent, how had he missed this?*

"I'm sorry Will." Dan was suffering. He betrayed his sister's secret and made his brother more miserable than he already was.

"You don't have to be sorry, son. It's not your fault. It's not anybody's fault. I don't expect you to stay children forever. I'm aware you're growing up, I just…I don't know, I just didn't want it to happen yet. Is it serious between them?"

"Yeah, pretty serious. He's a nice guy. He's smart, he's at Boalt you know, and he really cares about Jules."

"That's good." Will was still trying to take in the idea of his little girl having sex.

"It's not like they're going to get married or anything, I think they want to live together first…"

The second arrow! "She's going to *live* with him?"

"No! I mean, not *right* away." Dan couldn't believe the hole he was digging himself into. "I have to go, okay, I'll just take my bike to class." He got up from the table to leave, but the long arm of his brother pulled him back.

"Sit down, I'll drive you to class. I'm not mad at you. I'm not going to tell Jules, okay? This is between you and me."

Dan surveyed him with suspicion.

"I promise, it's man to man, sit down." He sank back onto the kitchen chair and they talked, Dan spilling what he knew about his sister's plans. There was an opening in Jason's house on Channing Street, a large, sunny room upstairs that another girl was giving up to move in with her boyfriend. Jules didn't want to tell Will because she didn't know how he would take it. He was already in such misery about Samantha, she couldn't bear to hurt him any more.

Will took it all in. His little girl was moving out. His family was scattering to the wind. Soon Dan would go too, and there would be no more generations to come, the rooms at the top of the stairs that had once been his father's, then his and Dave's, then filled again by Henry and Maria's next fold of children, would lie empty. He was too hopelessly irredeemable to provide the next occupants. It all ended with him—four generations, the fecund passion of his parents, all of it would be brought to a whimpering end.

"Let's go, I'll drop you off at school."

Dan searched his brother's eyes to get a read on how much damage he had caused. Will looked at his face and saw the little boy still trying to make everyone happy. He was touched that his children were trying to protect him from any more pain. He cupped his hand on Danny's head and kissed him. "Stop worrying, I can handle it. There's nothing to feel guilty about, okay? It was bound to happen sooner or later, I'm a big boy."

As they drove the short ride to the campus, Will felt his stomach tightening. He tried to focus on the road and not look too closely at the gaggles of students rushing to class, but they were so clueless about their own mortality they crisscrossed the narrow streets mindlessly, staring into their phones or chatting with friends, with no regard for traffic signs or oncoming cars, until he finally had to slam on the brakes mid street to avoid taking out two or three of them as they crossed against a light. As he did, from the corner of his eye, he saw her. First it was the reddish blonde hair, pulled behind her ears, the Fall breeze sending it flying as she futilely tried to keep it out of her eyes with a sweep of her hand. Then her face, her eyes turning toward the sound of the screeching brakes as she navigated with the crowd across the street. She had a bright yellow scarf wrapped around her neck against the cold, the book bag was strapped across her body between the curves of her breasts. At first she didn't see him through the throng of students, but then she caught sight of him and her gait slowed. Her face momentarily lost its animation and then…something flickered across it…sadness? She paused briefly in front of the car, locked in his gaze, as though she didn't know what to do next. He lifted his hand to wave to her, but just then someone crossed between them, jostling her and she began to walk again, turning her head back one last time to look at him. It all happened in an instant, but to Will it seemed in slow motion, her yellow scarf billowing in the wind and then disappearing back into the crowd. Finally, the car behind him honked, lurching him back to reality, and he accelerated to the next corner to drop Dan off. He pulled up to the curb and saw his boy staring at him.

"You still love her…" Dan said, taking in what had just happened. "And she loves *you*!"

"Go to class." Will said.

Dan grabbed his backpack and got out of the car. "You always tell me to listen to my gut. So what is your gut telling you now, Will?" He slammed the door hard and walked away from his brother without looking back. Will sat for a minute collecting himself.

Then he turned at the next corner and navigated the car to Mercy.

twenty-eight

"Hey, do you have time for lunch, I need to talk to you about something." It was Lee on the phone.

Will winced. "If it's the Samantha issue, I'm talked out." He was still trying to recover from his close encounter with her a week before.

"Don't be so self-absorbed, it's about me, I need some advice."

"Fine. I'm free at 12:30."

"Okay, I'll see you then."

Lee was already sitting at the table when Will walked up with his tray of food. They saw each other every day, but Lee was still surprised at how thin and worn his friend looked.

"Have you talked to Karen about the sleeping?"

"Yes."

"Because there's no reason not to take something until you get through this…"

"I'm aware."

"You sound like you've got a cold."

"I'm fine, what do you need advice about?"

"You sound pretty congested, are you sure you shouldn't go home?"

"I'm fine. The advice?"

"It's about Karen."

"You're asking *my* advice about a woman?"

Lee ignored him. "We've been dating exclusively for awhile now, you know staying at each others houses, toothbrushes, weekend clothes, that kind of thing, and I'm thinking of asking her to move in with me."

Will was stunned. "Wow. Really? I had no idea it was that serious between you two."

"Yeah, pretty damn serious. She's terrific, I don't want to lose her again."

The words stung. "Yeah, that would definitely be a mistake."

"So what do you think?"

"No."

"No? …Why?"

"Have you learned nothing from me? I'm like the ancient mariner walking around with a giant albatross around my neck. You're over forty, you can't be asking her for a half-ass commitment like that. What are you going to do, put up Ikea bookcases and walk her to geometry class? If there is one thing Carlotta has driven home to me it's that women in their thirties are not interested in half-ass commitments. You either man-up and ask her to marry you, or keep doing the back and forth thing to each other's houses until you grow a pair."

"Wow, I did not expect to hear that from you."

"Yeah. I'm Yoda now. Unfortunately my wisdom came a little too late."

"The thing is, I have some baggage, you know..."

Will looked exasperated. "Who are you talking to? I am the Maharajah of baggage. I could fly to the moon and back and never have to do laundry. Get over it and ask her to marry you before you lose her."

Lee tried to broach the subject of Sam again.

"Have you *tried* calling her?"

"No. I can't do that to her, I hurt her enough. I don't deserve her."

"Will..."

"I have to go." He pushed the tray of food away, uneaten, and got up to leave.

"At least eat some lunch, you look like you've lost twenty pounds. And take something for that cold, you sound awful."

"I don't have a cold, I don't get sick."

"God, you're stubborn."

"Don't ask her to move in."

"Yeah, yeah, I got it."

Will woke up the next morning feeling as though someone was sitting on his chest. He was drenched in sweat and his throat and lungs were on fire. He got out of bed to pee, but as soon as he stood up a wave of dizziness passed through him and he flopped back down on the bed, face down. *He was sick. Damn.* He picked up the cell to call Carlotta.

"Hey, I'm sick. Tell Matt to fill in for me, will you?"

"Wow, you sound terrible."

"Just get Matt to fill in for me, okay?"

"You're actually sick, I never thought I'd live to see the day."

"Don't enjoy it too much. I'll be back in tomorrow, I just need a day to recover."

"A day? Have you got a fever?"

"I don't know," he lied.

"Is it in your lungs?"

"Possibly."

"Dizzy, headache, aching all over?"

"Yeah…Carlotta can you just—"

"You've got the flu, you're not going to be better by tomorrow."

"I think I can be the judge of that. The last time I checked I'm the one who went to medical school."

"I'll call Matt and tell him you'll be out the rest of the week."

"God, you're exhausting…"

"Do you have meds? Want me to bring some over?" He thought about Carlotta seeing him in the shape he was in, he would never hear the end of it.

"No, thank you. I have everything I need."

"Is someone there with you?"

Will's head was starting to pound.

"Danny's here, he doesn't have class today, I'm good."

"Okay, call me if you need anything. Stay in bed and don't…" She was still talking when he clicked off. His head was banging so badly he had to put the phone down.

He crawled up to the pillow and lay there, face down in misery. He had to pee, but he couldn't imagine making it the whole distance to the bathroom. *So this was how it was going to end. Taken out by the common flu "…not with a bang but a whimper."*

He drifted off in a fevered stupor for a while, but the need to relieve his bladder woke him up again. He sat at the side of the bed and put his head between his knees to try to stop the dizziness, and finally managed to stumble to the bathroom. It was a herculean effort to stand long enough to finish the task, after which he slumped back into bed and launched into a fit of coughing.

"Will, are you okay?" It was Dan, hearing the coughing from his room down the hall.

"I'm fine son, don't come near me, I'm contagious."

Dan ignored him and walked into the room to check on him. "Wow, you're hot, you have a pretty high fever."

"I'm okay, can you just get me some ibuprofen? And some of that codeine cough medicine you had when you had bronchitis—do we still have it in the fridge?"

"Yeah, I think so, it might be expired though."

"Doesn't matter. And wash you your hands, I'm full of germs."

Dan disappeared downstairs and returned with the cough medicine and pills. "I brought you some juice too. You should drink lots of fluids." Will smiled at his boy all grown up, taking care of him. "Here's the spoon for the cough medicine, but it expired two months ago."

"No worries, it'll be fine. I don't need a spoon." Will cracked open the bottle and gulped it down.

"Nice measuring, Dr. Will." Dan smiled.

"Measuring is for amateurs." Will smiled back at him and dropped back down onto the pillow.

"I'll make you some chicken soup if you want."

"Thanks, babe, maybe later, I think I'm just going to sleep now."

"Okay, I'm home all day working on a paper, so I'll be here if you need me. I'll check in on you." When he checked on him later, Will was knocked out, raging with fever. Dan got the thermometer from the medicine cabinet and took his temperature. 103. He got a bowl of cool water and some washcloths and sat next to his brother wringing out the cloths and placing them on his forehead and neck to cool him off. "Your fever is really high, you need to take some more of this ibuprofen. It'll help."

"God that feels good," he said as Dan placed the cool cloth across his forehead.

"You always did this when I was sick, I remember how good it felt."

Will tried to focus his eyes on Dan. "Are you wearing glasses, or am I hallucinating?"

Dan smiled. "No, I'm wearing glasses. They prescribed 'em for all the video editing stuff. They're mild, but they help."

"They make you look very studious. Reminds me of when you were little. You had a pair of plastic sunglasses that you knocked the lenses out of and wore everywhere. You wanted to look just like Harry Potter. Then Jules wanted some, because she had to have everything just like you, so I bought her a pair of cheap sunglasses and knocked the lenses out, and for a couple of months the two of you walked around Berkeley that way. Everyone thought I was the father of two half-blind children until they realized there were no lenses." They both laughed, and Will broke into a coughing fit. "Oh shit, it hurts to laugh. Wow, I have more sympathy for my patients knowing what this feels like."

"Yeah, you've never really been sick before."

"I know, it's quite a revelation."

"You're still really hot. Let me put some more cold wash-cloths on you." He was running the cool cloth along the inside of Will's arm when he stopped short. "What's this?" He ran his finger along a small tattoo hidden on the inside curve of Will's upper right arm, peeking out under the sleeve of his t-shirt: *HDT♥MCG*. "I've never seen this before…"

"Really? I got that many years ago. Got drunk one night and Lee and I went to a tattoo parlor on Telegraph Ave. It's mom and dad's initials. Didn't want to forget them…like I *could*." He smiled.

Dan looked into his brother's eyes. "You still miss 'em, don't you."

"Yeah. Fifteen years, but I still miss 'em every day."

"I don't remember very much about them, Will, I feel bad. Sometimes I try to see their faces, but I can't."

"No, you don't have to feel bad, son, you were so little." He cupped his hand over his boy's head. "They had you for four years—really important years. They left their mark on you, I see it all the time in the things you do. Here, want to see something else?" He pulled up his other sleeve. In the same location, on his left arm, was another small tattoo: *JMT♥DDT*.

Dan looked at his brother with amazement. "Jules and me…I can't believe I never saw that before…"

"Maybe you *did* need glasses," he smiled. Then he saw Dan's wheels spinning. "Don't get any ideas. *No tattoos*, hear me? There are dirty needles and hepatitis and all kinds of bad shit out there. No tattoos!"

Dan smiled. "You'll never stop."

"No, I'll never stop worrying about you. Might as well accept it."

"I'm going to get some more juice for you."

"You're a good boy, I love you."

"I love you too."

"Do me a favor."

"Sure, what?"

"If I'm not better in a few days, smother me with this pillow, because I cannot live like this."

Dan laughed. "What a wuss."

Lee walked into the house and headed up the stairs to Will's room, meeting Dan in the hallway.

"Hey babe, I'm just checking on Will, how's he doing?"

"I'm not deaf." Will barked from his bed.

"Cranky as usual, I see."

"His fever is over 103 now."

"Is he taking anything?"

"Codeine cough medicine and ibuprofen. But the cough medicine is expired. He said it didn't matter. He's been drinking it."

"I see." Lee walked to Will's bed. "How you doing, cowboy?"

"I know now why I never get sick, it sucks."

"Yeah, sucks to find out you're mortal, doesn't it? It's a shock to all of us. I brought you some fresh cough medicine and a decongestant. Is your chest okay?"

"Yeah, except for the gallon of phlegm sitting on it."

"Can I listen to it?"

"No. If it gets any worse I'll diagnose myself."

"With 103 fever? That ought to be interesting. Do you need anything else?"

"No, I'm good. You didn't do that thing you said you were going to do, did you?"

"No, I took your advice and tabled that plan."

"Good. I'm okay then, thanks for stopping by."

"Sure you wont let me listen to your chest?"

"I'm sure."

"Okay. I'll check in on you later." He turned to Dan. "Call me if his fever goes any higher."

"Okay."

Dan was working on his paper when his phone lit up with a text. It was Will asking to bring him his stethoscope. He dutifully dug it out of the drawer in the hallway and brought it upstairs.

"Wouldn't it be better if Lee checked you out?"

"No, I've got it handled."

"You've been coughing all morning…"

"I'm fine, son, go work on your paper."

Lee was finishing with a patient when he saw Will's number light up on his phone.

"Hey, it's me. Can you prescribe me a z-pak, I've got bronchitis."

"Really. You diagnosed yourself?"

"Yeah."

"I can prescribe something for you, but not until I listen for myself."

"It's not rocket science, I listened to my chest, I have bronchitis."

"No drugs until I listen for myself."

"Fine. Just bring the azithromycin and you can listen yourself. I'll bet you twenty bucks it's bronchitis."

"That's a deal. I'll be there in an hour."

By the time Lee got there Will's fever was spiking again. Dan was sitting on the edge of the bed with the wet washcloths looking worried. Lee took advantage of Will's weakened state to examine him. He was definitely in trouble—high fever, swollen glands, raw throat and whopping congestion in both lungs—the months of stress were finally taking a toll.

"Well, cowboy, you owe me twenty bucks."

"Really? It's not bronchitis?"

"No. It's pneumonia. A whopping case of it too. I can hear crackling at the ribs, both sides. Stereo ear infections. I should take you in for an x-ray, but I don't want to drag you out in this weather with that fever. I'm going to start you on septra, you're out for a week --at least."

"I can't miss a week of work..."

"You don't have a choice, Will. You can't fool around with this, you're not superman. I'll call Carlotta."

Will dropped back on the pillow exhausted and beaten. His life was unraveling by the hour.

The following days were lost in a swirl of feverish hallu-cination. He saw his boy, tenderly draping the cool washcloths, Juliana bringing peonies, sitting on the edge of the bed read-ing to him. There was Eleanor, her voice full of concern, Lee and Dave and Carlotta appearing and disappearing, talking in hushed voices. He saw Miranda lying hurt on the gurney, and Samantha, her bright yellow scarf billowing in the wind, her face tinged with sadness. When the fever and fog finally lifted, he felt as though he had been hollowed out.

"Okay," Lee said, listening one last time to his lungs. "You're good to go back to work next week as long as your fever doesn't come back. Half days only, you're pretty wiped out. We'll get some more x-rays then. You've lost a lot of weight, you've got to start eating or I'm going to call in Maria to come and cook up some of her masterpieces."

Will was quiet. "Those were the days, right?" His voice trailed off with memories of meals around the kitchen table.

"Yes they were." Lee grew pensive.

"Jules is moving out next month."

"I heard."

"Danny will probably be close behind."

"I know. They're growing up. We knew it would happen one day." Lee got lost in his own memories.

"I'm thinking of giving up the house to Dave."

"What...?"

"Yeah, he's doing good with Alexa, you know, it seems pretty serious. He's got his head on straight now, I think it should go to him, he can fill it with a bunch of kids. I can move to a smaller place, near the hospital."

"Will..."

"Let's face it, I'm 42. I had my chance. I blew it. It's not meant to happen for me. I was lucky enough to raise Dan and

Jules, I got to see them grow up, and I'll get to watch them get married and have kids of their own. That'll make me happy."

Lee looked into Will's eyes and saw the vacant look of exhaustion he'd seen in patients so many times when they were spent from an illness. It was a loss of the divine spark that drives people to dream and plan and imagine a future. It pained him to see his friend's spirit so bankrupt.

"We'll talk about it tomorrow, okay?" He patted his arm." Get some sleep now."

"Okay." Will said. He dropped back down on the pillow, too weary to argue.

twenty-nine

"Welcome back, Will. It's great to see you." Karen had been warned by Lee, but she was still shocked by how pale and thin her patient looked. His clothes hung from him, his face was gaunt. "How are you feeling?"

"Much better. Happy to be back in the saddle. I'm not really good at laying around, as you can imagine, way too much time to think." Will fidgeted nervously and avoided her eyes as he sat down on the couch across from her chair.

"Where would you like to start today?"

"I don't know...wow. There's so much, it's hard to know where to begin." He held his head in his hands while he gathered his thoughts. "I guess the most important thing is Jules moving out. You probably heard." She could hear the pain in his voice.

"I did hear. So, let's start there. Tell me, how you're feeling about that."

"I understand, you know, she wants to spread her wings. She's grown up now—well, kind of." He rolled his eyes. "Jason is a good kid, they're crazy about each other. She's moving into his big house on Channing Street with four other students, so she's excited..." His voice trailed off. "It's just...*wow*. I don't know, I can't imagine my life without her, you know, she's my little girl... sitting curled up on the couch next to me watching baseball, all our talks over breakfast while she's putting on her makeup, the sound of her violin singing through the house...I think I'll miss that the most."

"It's hard for parents to watch their children leave, it's only natural you know."

"Yeah, I know—well, intellectually anyway. I just didn't think it would hurt this much. I mean it *physically* hurts." He clenched his fist over his heart to illustrate. "Do other people say that, because it's like *actual pain*."

"Many of my patients describe it that way."

"And pretty soon my boy will probably want to go too, and then what will I do?" He looked at her helplessly, as if he expected her to provide the answer, but she lobbed it back in his lap.

"Then...what *will* you do?"

"I have no idea." He slumped into the cushions. "I just don't...see a future."

"What about your *own* future?"

"No, I can't see that...I think my heart will just break." He went silent, looking up at the ceiling. "I'm so terrified of losing them, sometimes late at night I try to imagine what it will be like when they're gone...I try to see ahead, but it's all just dark."

"Why do you think it scares you so much, Will?"

He thought hard for a minute, staring into the nothing-ness. "I guess...I don't want to be the only one left in that house with the memories of my parents. I don't want be the only one who remembers them." He felt the tears well in his eyes.

Karen had waited a long time for the right moment to ask him the next question, and now at last, looking at his pale and thin frame slumped into the couch, she knew it was time.

"Do you think...maybe you haven't finished saying good-bye to your parents?" The silence was thick between them for several minutes before he raised his eyes up to look at her.

"There was no *time*. I was so busy trying to take care of the kids and do my residency...there was no time for anything else...I had to keep moving, you know, I had to keep everyone whole, that was my job, that was my promise to my parents. I couldn't let Dan and Jules see how broken I was, how much we all lost when they died..."

Karen pushed further. "Do you ever think about that, Will? About them...dying?"

He winced at the word and went silent again, retrieving the painful memories as he had so many times before, as if he was fishing them out of a trunk that always sat near him, cracked open, waiting for him to examine its contents again and again.

"Sometimes I dream about it when I'm half asleep at night. Their car swerving and crashing on the wet road, the sound of breaking glass, the roaring of the fire. I wonder if they were unconscious or if they were afraid, suffering, lying in the dark and cold and rain waiting for help. Did they call out to each other? Did they call out to their children halfway around the world? I wonder if the paramedics came fast enough, if they talked to them, if they treated them tenderly. Did they separate them when they brought them into the hospital? Did they get to say goodbye to each other?" He stared at Karen as if for an answer, but she remained silent. He dug deeper into the memories. "When we got the report, it said my mother died first, and my father died in surgery…if he knew she was gone did he even fight to survive, or did his heart just give out at the thought of his life without her? Did the doctors try hard enough to save them? Did they know how much they loved each other…that their children were waiting for them to come home? Did they know my mother could make a violin sing so sweetly it brought people to tears, and when she died no one would ever hear that sound again?" He looked at Karen plaintively. "I can never hear that sound again…"

"There was nothing you could have done, Will. They were halfway around the world. You couldn't have saved them."

"That's not true…you *know*!" He went silent again. She waited, watching him struggle before he could utter the next words.

"Tell me why you think you need redemption, Will."

He stiffened on the couch as though he might get up to leave, but then his body sank back into the cushions. He stared at her, his eyes filled with pain.

"*I'm* the one. I'm the one who let them get on that plane. I put their luggage into the car—I drove them to the airport, and I kissed them goodbye, and I let them walk down that ramp, arm-in-arm, to die." He closed his eyes, his whole body pierced with anguish as he remembered the smell of his mother's perfume and the touch of her lips on his cheek, his father holding her waist smiling back at him. It was all so vivid in front of him, he reached his hand out to pull them back.

"It wasn't your fault, Will." Karen's voice was soft.

He opened his eyes and stared at her, trying to parse the words, his hand still outstretched, grasping thin air.

"You couldn't have saved them."

His body began to shake. The quivering rumbled up from the deepest part of him, slowly at first and then like an avalanche, gaining intensity until he couldn't pull it back or control it. He began to sob, his body giving in to the years of suppressed pain. He wept without self-consciousness and without any sense of time or place, as though fifteen years of tears were welled up in him. He wept for his parents and for himself, for all the hurt and frightened souls who had suffered in his presence, for every wretched, broken being he had tried to rescue and failed.

Karen got up to sit next to him on the couch and put her arm around him to comfort him. He slumped next to her, exhausted and shaking for a long time. And then, at last, it stopped. Whether he was too spent to feel or was finally done saying goodbye to his parents, he didn't know, but an odd sense of peace filled the hollowed-out parts of him as it never had before. Peace and resignation.

"Maybe it's time for you to think about your own life now. Maybe you're finally ready."

"I don't know." He suddenly felt a weariness and starvation deep in his bones. "I don't think I have anything…I don't think there's a life left for me."

Karen saw the fatigue overtaking him.

"You've been through a lot in the last few months. You're tired, and you need time to take it all in. We'll talk more next time. Maybe next time we can talk about the *future*."

"Okay."

"Because you do have a future, Will, you just haven't looked for it yet."

He looked into her eyes, at the familiar, feminine face that had become his touchstone when he was in pain. She was his shaman, and she believed in him so unfailingly, he didn't have the heart to let her down. "Okay, if you say so." He said. He hugged her gently and collected himself. He was exhausted, but he felt strangely calm. He got up from the couch and walked back down the stairs to the ER.

When he got to his office Carlotta was standing over her desk shuffling papers absently. She looked up at him with thinly disguised worry.

"I'm fine. You can stop pretending to be busy. It's late, go home."

She peered into his worn eyes. "Do you need a hug?"

He looked back at her affectionately. They had seen so much during their years together in the ER—the pain and capriciousness of life. In many ways she knew the landscape of his soul better than any woman.

"I wouldn't turn it down."

She hugged him tightly, the warmth of her ample body enveloping him.

"The Lord does not give us more than we can handle." He felt the power of her strong arms around him and he didn't want her to let go of him. He felt as if his body would fly apart into pieces like an empty husk.

"We'll see." He said, holding onto her. "We'll see."

thirty

For the first time in all the years of raising Dan and Jules, Will ceded Thanksgiving to Dave, sending the three of them off to Oakhaven without him. While they dined to chamber music, feasting on a seven course meal under the blissful watch of the fresco seraphim, he stretched out on the sofa mindlessly watching endless hours of college football bowls, picking at a turkey dinner Dave had prepared for him and left in the fridge. He was considering working the evening shift to give another doctor the night off, but he was still fighting fatigue from the pneumonia and Lee convinced him otherwise.

Lee was having dinner with Karen Winslow and her family, another testament to how serious their relationship had become. He stopped by to check on Will before he left, dressed nattily in a new sports jacket and slacks he had bought for the occasion.

"This is a new look for you." Will said, surveying the hand-stitched jacket and Italian polo sweater underneath. You look pretty damn smooth."

"Yeah, I thought it was time to lose the college frat boy look now that I'm in an actual relationship with a grown-up."

"Good for you."

"You going to be okay here alone?"

"Are you kidding? I've got the house to myself, Dave made me a fantastic dinner, and I don't have to deal with interrogation from Eleanor, I'm in hog heaven. I may milk this recovery 'till Christmas."

"You're still taking the antibiotics?"

"Yeah, I have a few days left."

"Don't get cocky, the last x-ray showed you're still not clear."

"I know."

"Okay, enjoy football."

"Will do. Behave yourself. Don't blow it, you're almost at the finish line."

Lee laughed. "I'll try."

With the rare luxury of time on his hands, Will decided to make some Thanksgiving calls. He called Carlotta, who managed to give him a pep talk in spite of the fact her large, boisterous family and the football game blasting on her big-screen TV made it almost impossible to carry on a conversation. He called Maria at Margarita's farm in Gilroy, where he could hear Jorge playing Mariachi music in the background as Maria put every member of the Gonzales family on the phone to wish him

Happy Thanksgiving, including Margarita's newest grandchild, who gurgled into the receiver and then promptly hung up. He called Miranda, who was still recovering but already back to working from her glass castle, no doubt terrorizing anyone unfortunate enough to be at the receiving end of her legal prowess. He even toyed briefly with the idea of texting Samantha to say Happy Thanksgiving, but he decided against it. He wondered what she was doing--maybe gone back to Maine to spend time with her mother. Or maybe she had moved on to a new relationship, maybe she was having Thanksgiving dinner with *him*, dressed in that beautiful black dress, smelling of lavender, her hair pulled up showing the soft nape of her neck. The thought of her with another man made his chest ache.

He laid back on the couch and let the fatigue wash over him, drifting in and out of sleep, the roar of the games on television occasionally waking him up. By the time everyone arrived back home, he was in bed asleep. He woke briefly to hear their voices noisily chattering away downstairs, but he felt strangely detached from them, as though he had crossed over to another world, a solitary, isolated world where he was not part of the busy ebb and flow of the household he had once commanded.

As the weeks rolled on and Christmas approached, his strength slowly returned. Gathering the Thompkins family in the hallway at the foot of the stairs for the annual Christmas Eve extravaganza at Oakhaven, he began to feel a little of the old spark in himself.

"Everyone down here in five minutes or I'm leaving without you." He yelled to the top of the stairs for the third time. He turned to Jason, who was dressed in a suit and tie waiting patiently for Juliana in the living room.

"You clean up very nicely." Will smiled at him.

"Thanks Doc." Jason looked down at the floor, gathering his nerve. "Listen, I know this is a really important night, going to your grandmother's. Jules told me you're under a lot of pressure for everything to go just right. So, I want you to be honest when I ask you this." He looked directly at Will.

"Okay, shoot."

"You know I'm crazy about Jules, and I would do anything to make her happy. But do you think this is the right time to confront your grandmother with our relationship, considering…you know…the ethnicity factor and all?"

Will was touched by his honesty. He put his hand on the young man's shoulder and locked his eyes on him. "That is a very thoughtful question, son. I appreciate your directness. Here's my answer: You're a good man, and you're Jules' choice. If your ethnicity is a problem for my grandmother, she can kiss my ass. Okay?"

"Okay," Jason laughed. "Just wanted to make sure."

"Jules, Dan, NOW." Will yelled out.

"Coming!" Juliana stood in front of him "I'm ready."

"Are you wearing *that*?" Will stared at her strapless dress

"Yes, why?"

"It's a little revealing, isn't it?"

"Will, I'm not eight years old. Did you expect me to wear a plaid dress with a big bow?"

"You look gorgeous, Jules." Jason chimed in.

"Thank you." She smiled sweetly at him, brushing Will aside.

Dan came bounding down the stairs and stood in front of Will. "I'm ready."

"You couldn't shave just this once to spare me the grief of listening to your grandmother?" Will said, staring at his stubble.

"I'm not shaving for grandma."

"Okay, then you spend the entire night bragging about your grades."

"Agreed."

"You can skip the squeaker in biology."

"Got it."

"And *you*," he turned back to Jules, "leave your sweater on until we get in and I get a drink, I don't care if the butler tries to take it, tell him you're cold."

"Got it."

"Diamond earrings from your grandmother?"

"Yes, look." She offered her ears for perusal. "Okay," he turned to Dan. "Are you wearing the gold cufflinks she gave you?"

"Check." Dan held his sleeves out as Will examined them.

"This isn't a French cuff shirt, how did you get those in there?"

"I couldn't find that shirt, so I poked a hole next to the button with my penknife. Ingenious, right?"

Will looked exasperated. "Did I teach you nothing?" He looked at the unruly curls, now cut short but still managing to look disheveled. "Did you even comb your hair?"

"Yes, it's combed."

"Okay, you know the drill. Compliment everything, and reveal no family secrets."

"Check."

"Check."

"Check."

As they entered through the Oakhaven gate, Will felt the familiar flush of anxiety and nostalgia. The oaks standing sentry on the road leading to the house had lost most of their leaves for the winter, making their silvery trunks, lit by spotlights, look even more austere and beautiful, like sculpted giants. The old stone house was magnificently aglow for the season, every tree and shrub glittered with tiny twinkling white lights. Red and green lights lit up the roof and eaves; animated reindeer pranced along the roof. Outside, costumed Dickens carolers were greeting the guests. He looked over at Dan and Jules and saw their faces glowing with anticipation.

They got out of the car and spontaneously lined up for one last inspection before going in. Will eyed them affectionately, all grown up, still obediently fulfilling the ritual they'd performed for him so many years. They were almost 20 now, but they were still his children. He patted down Dan's hair and adjusted his tie. "Stand up straight." He buttoned Juliana's sweater to cover her strapless dress. "Keep the sweater on till we get past her." He smiled at Jason, lined up with the others looking nervous. "And you," he patted his cheek, "Try to look a little less ethnic."

Jason grinned. "Will do doc."

"Okay, we're going in."

Eleanor greeted them at the door, the carolers parting like the Red Sea as she stepped out onto the front portico, draped fabulously in a black silk gown splattered with huge red chrysanthemums.

"There are my loves!" She threw her arms around Dan and Jules covering them with kisses as they soaked up her affection. "Look at you, so grown up. You're beautiful, just beautiful," she beamed. Will could see she was probably a few glasses of champagne in already, but the affection was genuine. Eleanor loved her grandchildren more deeply than anything in her life, as opulent and blessed as it was. He smiled when he saw how happy she was to see them. "And you must be Jason." She hugged him warmly. "Welcome to Oakhaven, I'm very pleased to meet you. Anyone who makes my little Juliana happy makes me happy too."

Will held back as he always did while she ushered Dan and Jules inside. Then Eleanor surprised him by turning around to greet him as he stood alone in the entryway.

"My darling." She said, cupping his face tenderly in her hands and kissing him gently on both cheeks. "I've been so worried about you, I'm so happy to see you."

Will felt tears begin to well in his eyes. He was embarrassed to let his guard down in front of his old opponent, but he was so raw, he couldn't hold them back. He hugged his grandmother tightly, trying to avoid her seeing the emotion in his face. "I'm happy to see you too." He said. And for a long minute, he let her hold him, not wanting to leave her embrace.

She linked her arm in his and pressed him close as she ushered him inside. The house was glowing, the smell of turkey and roast and other delicacies wafted up from underneath the silver domes lined up on the buffet table and from trays of food being whirled through the room by waiters in tuxedos. The enormous blue spruce Christmas tree rose up three stories between the twin stairwells, spectacular with its shimmering silver and gold lights and its giant colored glass ornaments—teddy bears, dolls, toys, angels and Santa Clauses all jostling for space in a cacophony of religious and pagan splendor. And of course, as always, there was the explosion of brightly wrapped presents spilling out from underneath, nearly tripping the guests as they circumvented them on their way into the dining room.

Will felt a creeping sense of joy overtake him. He thought of his father and mother, chiding his grandmother for her excess while they ate and danced and watched their children's eyes light up as they ripped open the packages. "Too much, mom!" Henry Thompkins always said, but now Will understood that it *wasn't* too much, none of it was too much. Their lives were so brief that every Christmas they had together was a gift worthy of any amount of wealth Eleanor Simpson Thompkins Ross could lavish celebrating it. Maybe she was wiser than all of them.

Before he could get to the bar to order a drink, a waiter materialized with a silver tray holding a single, generously poured glass of scotch. Will smiled and lifted it from the tray. He downed a long sip and walked to where Dan and Jules were already mingling with the guests, many of them young, and others who were Eleanor's long-time friends. He stood back watching the two of them talking and laughing easily. They were as at home here in the opulence of Atherton as they were in Berkeley.

His father had gotten his wish. Suddenly he felt an arm wrap around him, pulling him close. He turned to see Eleanor beside him, gazing wistfully at her grandchildren from the edge of the crowd.

"They're wonderful, aren't they? Just perfect."

"They are."

"I wish your father could have seen them all grown up, he would be so proud of them."

Will saw a sadness flicker across her face and he wrapped his arm tightly around her. He felt, for the first time, her frailty, disguised by the jewels and expanse of black silk and fiery chrysanthemums, as if age and grief were finally catching up to her.

"I'll tell you a secret." She said quietly. "Sometimes, when I can't bear the thought that he's left me, I imagine him out in the cosmos—not in heaven, you know how he would feel about that—watching over us all, surrounded by his beloved books, with your mother playing Puccini next to him. It's terribly sentimental I know, but it makes me happy to think of them that way."

Will looked down at her and kissed her cheek. "I'll tell *you* a secret." He squeezed her tightly. "I do the same thing." They stood silently at the edge of the crowd for a few minutes caught in their own memories as they watched the festivities.

"Do you remember that little bronze statue of Hermes Dad kept on his desk?" Will asked.

"I do, we bought it on a trip to Greece when he was about 12. He always said it was his favorite Greek god, I never knew why."

"I looked him up once. Hermes was the son of Zeus. He was the patron of travelers, known for his helpfulness to mankind—kind of like Saint Christopher but the agnostic version." They both laughed at Henry Thompkins's eschewing of any religious baggage. "He helped guide Perseus on his quest to slay Medusa by loaning him his magic sandals which gave Perseus the ability to fly. When I was raising the kids, I always felt as if Dad was my Hermes. I could hear him whispering in my ear, advising me what to do, intervening miraculously when things got tough. It got me through a lot of hard times."

Eleanor squeezed his hand, delighted to hear a new revelation about her son. "That must make me Medusa." She grinned wickedly, and they both burst into laughter. "Well as long as we're telling secrets," her voice softened, "I'll tell you another one. You were right to keep them in Berkeley. It's where they belonged, in that old house surrounded by the memories of Henry and Maria and the world they loved. Your father would be proud of you for the way you raised them." She kissed him. "*I'm* proud of you." And in a moment she was gone, the red chrysanthemums evaporating into the crowd of guests.

Will was stunned. He couldn't remember a time when she had let her guard down so completely, when they weren't locked in battle. He felt released, as though the eternal game of chess had finally come to a close. He stood in the center of the living room and raised his eyes up to the blissful faces of the seraphim gazing down on the human revelers. They looked resplendent, their pastel countenances and feathered wings lit by the glow of Christmas lights and candles from below. He heard the noise of the crowd as they erupted into a spontaneous sing-along while the band played *God Rest Ye Merry Gentlemen*. He watched

Jules impishly snatch the violin from one of the musicians and begin to play along, the notes rising in the air and drifting back on the revelers. He raised his eyes to the seraphim again, and all at once he understood. They weren't blindly ignorant of the ebb and flow of happiness and pain that played out beneath them. They weren't mocking the hapless mortals below who were powerless to stop their own suffering. They were simply *accepting it.* Accepting, that in spite of all of its capriciousness and sorrow, life was a joyful enterprise—sweet and sad and all too fleeting, but filled with grace. Mono no aware.

Suddenly the sight and smell of food from the buffet table assaulted his senses. He felt an overpowering hunger, as if he hadn't eaten in 15 years. He dove into the gleaming silver chafing dishes of delicacies, filling his plate with pork roast and gravy, turkey and potatoes, caviar and salmon and duck piled high in a wild mélange of succulent flavors. He couldn't get enough of it, every bite seemed to be a revelation in his mouth. He was *starving.*

Jules and Dan looked over at him from the living room, stunned to see him with a huge plate of food, stabbing hungrily into a slab of roast with a fork. They broke away from the crowd to check on him.

"Is everything okay?" Dan asked, surveying his brother's face for signs of trouble. "What did grandma say to you?"

"Everything is fine. She was just telling me how proud she was of you. No worries. Have you tasted this food?" Will said, his mouth still full, "It's *amazing.* She really outdid herself this time, it's fantastic, like nothing I've ever tasted before," he popped a lobster puff pastry in his mouth and savored its buttery sweetness.

They stared at him in disbelief. "I'm glad you're enjoying it, it's nice to see you eating," Jules said tentatively as he dove into a heaping breast of duck soaked in gravy. "Are you...*sure* everything is okay?" They had seen so much bizarre behavior from their brother of late, neither of them was confident about how to assess his state of mind. Will held the plate of food with one hand and with the other pulled each one of his children toward him, planting a fragrant, greasy kiss on their foreheads. "*No te preocupes. Todo estará bien.*" He said, putting another bite of duck in his mouth. "Go, have fun."

With that, they obediently returned to the festivities, glancing back quizzically at Will still reveling in gastronomic excess. They didn't want to do or say anything that would stop his flow of nourishment at last.

Back home at the end of the evening, Will shed his clothes and dropped into bed. He heard Dan and Jules noisily scatter to their rooms, Jules still enough his little girl that she wanted to be home for Christmas morning. He heard Max clicking back and forth down the worn oak hallway trying to decide, with the rare luxury of a full house, whose bed he would sleep in.

He listened as the old house grew quiet, its wooden beams and struts creaking as they settled into the night. His eyes traced the outlines of the framed portraits on the wall across from his bed. It was too dark to see them clearly, but it didn't matter, he knew each one by heart. There, on the left, was Maria—Jules and Danny at her side. Next to her was Lee, grinning at the 'Sold" sign on his front lawn. On the right, he and Dave with their freshly-caught fish shimmering in the sunlight, their father standing proudly behind. And in the center…the black and white photo of his parents, young and vibrant, their arms entwined, their faces gleaming with passion. All of them were so dear, smiling out at him, held safely in time. And there, on the right, was a newly hung portrait, glancing back at him over her shoulder, her reddish-blonde hair tied in a crazy knot, her blue eyes fixed on him. *The memory of possibilities…*

He picked up the phone and pressed in the number.

"Samantha…it's Will."